OUT *of the* WILDERNESS

OUT *of the* WILDERNESS
DEB VANASSE

CLARION BOOKS
New York

Clarion Books
a Houghton Mifflin Company imprint
215 Park Avenue South, New York, NY 10003
Text copyright © 1999 by Deb Vanasse

The text is set in 12/17 Meridien.

Printed in the USA.

Library of Congress Cataloging-in-Publication Data
Vanasse, Deb.
Out of the wilderness / by Deb Vanasse.
p. cm.
Summary: Josh tries to endure living in the Alaskan wilderness
with his father and half-brother Nathan, but Nathan's
uncompromising reverence for nature and its wild creatures causes
difficulties that reinforce Josh's determination to return to city life.
ISBN 0-395-91421-3
[1. Fathers and sons—Fiction. 2. Brothers—Fiction.
3. Wilderness survival—Fiction. 4. Alaska—Fiction.] I. Title.
PZ7.V26244Ou   1999
[Fic]—dc21   98-22692
                                                       CIP
                                                       AC

QBP   10   9   8   7   6   5   4   3   2   1

to Tim,
who introduced me to the wilderness

—D.V.

OUT *of the* WILDERNESS

1

$\mathcal{T}$HE OCTOBER WIND blew down from the Alaska Range, rattling the dried yellow birch leaves until they fluttered to the ground. Hiking behind his father, Josh felt the cold sting hit his face like a slap.

As he picked his way through the brush, Josh listened to the crunching of leaves under his father's eager stride and his own steady step. Far behind on the trail, he could hear his half brother Nathan's light gait. It was a forlorn sound, Josh thought, a final farewell to summer, as the once healthy leaves were ground beneath their boots, to be soon buried beneath layer upon layer of snow.

Beyond the sound of their footsteps, there was silence. Sometimes the quiet of the wilderness bothered Josh more than anything else.

Abruptly the sound of his father's footsteps ceased. Instinctively Josh stopped, too, and looked up to see his father pointing toward a clearing.

The sound of Nathan's footsteps grew closer. Josh turned back and raised a gloved finger to his lips, but Nathan's eyes were on the trail. *Look up*. Josh spoke the words in his head. He dared not speak them out loud. If his father was pointing at a bull moose big enough to shoot, Josh's voice would spook the animal and ruin what could well be their last chance to have meat before winter set in.

Nathan's footsteps would spook it, too. Despite his thin frame, each step resounded as he drew nearer, announcing their presence. *Look up,* Josh willed again. The pain in his stomach, reminding him that they'd been on the trail for hours since breakfast, made the matter more urgent.

Not that they were starving. Not yet, anyway. But they were down to dried fish and berries and rice. Nathan had said they should be satisfied with that. People all over the world survived on less.

Nathan's steps came closer and closer to giving them away. His brother might be an adult, but sometimes he acted younger than Josh, insisting on foolish ideas that defied the laws of nature. Ideas like living on berries and rice, after the fish ran out.

It was only at his father's urging that Nathan had come along on their hunt. Maybe now, if his brother scared off an animal because he wasn't being careful, his father would realize that they didn't have to drag Nathan into everything they did.

Josh glanced ahead at his father. He stood in the same spot, no longer pointing but with one finger at his lips and the other motioning them forward.

Behind him, Josh heard Nathan's footsteps stop at last. He turned to face his brother, just a few feet back, and repeated his father's signals to come forward quietly. Josh felt a wave of irritation as he looked into Nathan's brown eyes staring back from his gaunt face.

Nathan could look sad about nothing and everything, especially when they were in the woods, and especially when they were hunting. His eyes said the words his mouth had repeated far too often, as far as Josh was concerned. They were intruding on the wilderness. Yet it had been Nathan's idea to leave the city behind and live off the land a hundred miles from Anchorage. The way Josh saw it, they had to intrude, if that's what shooting something meant, or the unforgiving wilderness would intrude on them in a big way.

Josh turned and picked his way slowly and carefully through the leaves to the place where his father stood. A smell of decay, stronger than the familiar autumn scent of rotting leaves and rose hips, surrounded them. Ahead in the clearing lay the remains of a moose, a moose they could have been cutting and caching had fortune dealt them a better hand. Instead, they stared at a black bear, its muzzle deep in the kill.

Josh felt a rush of adrenaline surge through his body. "Can you get a good shot?" he whispered.

"I think so," his dad whispered back. "He's busy with that carcass and upwind of us to boot. Hasn't even looked up. Think he's big enough?"

Josh studied the bear. Fifty yards in the distance, it was hard to gauge its size. But against the remains of the moose, it looked to be a little over four feet long.

"Second-year cub, I'll bet," Josh whispered. "Maybe one of those two that prowled around all summer with their mother."

Josh's dad tugged at the sling that held his rifle on his back, lifting the gun over his head. Each movement was studied and careful. Josh saw the sweat beading up along his brow, in spite of the wind. His father's years of hunting back in Wisconsin, when he was Josh's age and younger, all came together in moments like this.

Josh admired his father's steady arm, his controlled breathing, as he brought the rifle to his shoulder and set his sights on the bear. His own hunting experience was limited to the past year and a half they'd spent at Willow Creek, living in the wilderness, killing rabbits and ptarmigan, eventually learning to hit more than he missed. He was glad for his father's steady finger on the trigger right now.

"What do you think you're doing?"

The voice rang out from just behind them and echoed back from the hills in the distance. The bear reared up on its hind legs with a grunt, sniffing at the air. It opened its mouth, releasing an eerie series of woofs, primitive sounds like those a cowering dog would make. But the bear wasn't cowering. It stood erect, its black coat gleaming.

His father had told him, had told him and Nathan countless times, that a bear woofs just before it charges: before it charges to protect its young, before it charges to protect its food. The smell of decay seemed to suddenly overpower them. Had the wind picked up? The thought came to Josh as if through a fog.

"Shoot, Dad," he urged in a loud whisper. He could feel Nathan upon them, could see his arm reach forward to topple the rifle.

At the same time, a shot rang out and the rifle clattered to the ground at Josh's feet. The slow blur of his thoughts turned into a rush of action as the bear dropped to all fours and charged toward them, a bounding bundle of black fur. Nathan pushed between Josh and his father, throwing his father off balance. His father tumbled over a fallen log, and Nathan reached for the rifle.

Dazed, Josh grabbed for it, too. His grip tightened on the stock as Nathan pulled at the barrel. A thick scent clouded the air. Bear. Nathan had never shot at any animal, not even a rabbit. Josh tugged harder at the rifle, freeing it from Nathan's hands.

Nathan stared at the approaching bear, mesmerized. Their father crouched where he had fallen. It was the play-dead stance, the one he had told them to use if a bear ever attacked and they didn't have a gun. But at this moment, Nathan seemed oblivious, and Josh had a gun.

"The trees!" his father yelled from the ground. Did he mean run or climb? Josh's question half formed itself as he raised the rifle and found the charging bear in the sights. Through the scope, everything seemed to be shaking, and he couldn't get a steady fix. Now the bear looked huge, monstrous. Its teeth were bared and blood flecked its fur where it had wallowed in the moose carcass.

Twenty yards. Fifteen. Ten. As he pulled the trigger, Josh was aware only of the pounding of his own heart.

2

*T*HE SHARP CRACK OF THE SHOT left Josh's ears ringing. Through the scope, he could see the fury in the bear's eyes. Josh's heart beat wildly. Steady, he told himself. You have another shot if you need it.

With trembling fingers, he reached for the bolt of the gun. Then, in a split second, he saw a dazed, almost sad look overcome the animal. A sense of recognition nudged Josh through the panic, as if he had seen those eyes before. Then came a flood of relief as the charging bear faltered, stumbled, and rolled to its side five feet in front of him.

Josh stood, frozen, watching the mound of fur for any signs of movement.

He felt a hand on his shoulder. "Shot him stone cold dead," his father said. "I'm proud of you, Josh."

Josh took a deep breath and steadied himself. He felt more shaken than proud. The lifeless form that lay before him seemed another creature entirely from the charging mass of angry bear that could have emerged the victor from the attack. For a moment, Josh pictured himself as the bear, lifeless on the ground, blood pooling up beneath him.

He felt his father's hand lift from his shoulder. "Nate, if you don't play dead, you gotta go for the trees. Climb and hang on for dear life. And how you got so excited that you knocked that rifle from my hands I'll never know. Moves like that, and we won't be just playing dead." His father's tone was too light for his serious words.

So his father thought Nathan had just gotten excited and knocked the rifle from his hands. An accident. Josh looked at Nathan, who was staring at the dead bear as if he had come under some kind of spell. His brother had done strange things before. His rash move today was an unlikely accident.

If his father had any doubts, they weren't apparent. He ignored Nathan's stony silence and continued, "Well, bear meat's as good as moose, I guess. A little fish taste maybe, after a summer of feeding on salmon, but it'll get us through the winter." His father knelt beside the bear, spreading out the carcass, examining the shot.

"Almost five feet long, he was. Must be a second-year cub, all right."

Something flickered beyond Nathan's stare, a flashing of defiance. Josh had seen it before, at times when Nathan had challenged their father.

His father went on smiling, studying the carcass. "Looks like my shot was high in the shoulder, just enough to aggravate him. But you got him right through the chest."

"Then you're both to blame." Nathan's voice was deep, almost a growl.

Their father stood. "Blame? This is meat for the winter. That's what we came for."

"Not we. You. And you came for moose. Not bear. Not this cub." Nathan fairly shook with the words.

"Nate, let's be reasonable. We have to eat, moose or bear. And this bear was charging, remember?"

"You intruded." There was Nathan's favorite line. "It was protecting its food."

His father took a step closer to Nathan. "And we were protecting ourselves."

Nathan held out his arms and stepped backward, as if keeping an invisible shield between himself and his father. "This time you've gone too far. You've killed a brother."

"A brother? Nathan, this is your brother." He pointed at Josh. Josh looked down at his scuffed boots and the barrel of the rifle growing cold in his hand. He felt a knot forming in his stomach. His father's voice was steady, soothing, as it was whenever he tried to calm Nathan.

"This—" Josh looked up to see his father swing his pointing finger back at the bear "—is just an animal. We meant to get a moose. We got a bear. No difference."

Nathan pulled at his scraggly brown beard, as he often did when he was agitated. "Big difference. You said yourself it's one of the cubs we've seen all summer. I watched it fish for salmon with its mother. Watched it wrestle with its brother. Watched it forage for berries. I watched it until I knew it was no more an animal than I am."

Josh stared at the bear, remembering its charging fury. How could Nathan claim kinship with such an animal?

"Nate, even if you felt that one bear was special, we don't know for sure that this is the same bear."

"It's the same bear, all right. One of the cubs. You don't get it, do you? I've studied this sow and her cubs. I know where they feed and when. I know their grunts and their walks. I know every mark on their faces. Look there." He pointed at the muzzle of the dead animal. "That scar by his nose. His brother did that when they were just yearlings."

Josh could barely see a jagged scar beneath the whiskers on the bear's snout. The pounding in his chest had ceased, and he felt drained, wanting nothing more than to be transported far from his brother's raving. He turned away from the bear, away from Nathan and his father, and looked across the clearing, above the treetops, where a lone eagle circled in the gray sky. Through the wash of emotion, a thought came to him: Nathan knows this bear better than he knows me. Better than he wants to know me. Better than I want to know him.

"Let's be reasonable, here, Nate," Josh heard his father saying. When he turned to look, he saw Nathan backing farther away from his father's outstretched hand.

"I've had enough." Nathan's voice was loud but uneven against the wind. He backed toward the woods. "This isn't going to work."

"What isn't going to work?"

"Living with you and your indiscriminate killing." The wind swallowed Nathan's words, making them faint and distant.

"It has to work. You can't survive on your own out here." The redness rising in his father's face betrayed his frustration, but he kept his steady, even tone.

"Watch me!" His face set with determination, Nathan turned and strode into the woods.

"Nathan!" his father called after him, but Nathan kept walking. Josh tried to summon some emotion, some sense of urgency or regret. But he felt only an emptiness. He looked up again, searching for the eagle. It made one final, banking turn and glided toward the top of a towering spruce that swayed in the wind. With precision, its talons clasped the uppermost branch. There it sat, regally surveying the wilderness that stretched out in all directions. It had only to spread its massive wings and be gone, never to return.

Josh's father stood staring at the woods where his older son had retreated. Josh stepped to his side.

"He'll be all right, Dad. Just let him get this out of his system."

His father shook his head. "I hope so. Seems like nothing I do or say lately pleases him."

Josh knew the feeling. Everybody liked Nathan when they first met him. But once you got to know him, you figured out that the same high standards he set for himself he extended to everyone else. Josh tried to ignore Nathan's outbursts. But his father took them to heart. He had searched five years to find Nathan. Five years of moving from city to city, traveling ever westward, until finally they had found him in Anchorage.

His father had held fast to Nathan from that moment on, clinging like the eagle to the branch of the swaying tree. He had embraced Nathan's dream of living in the wilderness as if it were his own. As if Josh, the son who had been with him all along, mattered not in the least.

Perhaps if Nathan made good on his promise to head out on his own, his father would abandon the wilderness idea and they could return to a more normal life. The tiny hope fluttered to rest, like a falling birch leaf, atop Josh's thoughts.

"Let's take care of the bear," Josh said. "Let Nathan take care of himself."

His father shook his head. "I can't just let him go off on his own, angry like that. I didn't know he felt that way about this bear."

Josh stepped closer to his father. "How could you have known?" Josh reasoned. "Just give him some time to cool off. You know how he likes to be alone. It'll only make him madder if you go after him now."

His father stared again in the direction Nathan had gone. "I guess you're right. He'll get over it. Can't mess with that independent streak of his."

In silence, father and son set to the task of dressing the animal. As he watched his father's gleaming knife slice the carcass from tail to chin, Josh detached himself the way he had learned to do whenever there was an animal to be skinned or dressed. You had to forget that minutes before, this had been a living, breathing creature. You had to look at it clinically, as a coroner or mortician must look at a cadaver. You had to see the animal this way, or you couldn't survive. It wasn't fun or easy, but it was the way of the wilderness.

Josh knelt on one knee, pulling back the skin as his father carved it free from the thick layer of fat underneath. It was always Josh who helped his father with the skinning and butchering. Since their first day at Willow Creek, Nathan had neither killed an animal nor helped to skin one.

But he had said he respected the need to do so. For the first few months, he'd even eaten as they had. More recently, though, he'd refused all red meat. And now there was this business with the bear.

Josh helped his father pull the warm guts from the carcass, making a pile on the ground beside them. He wondered whether his father understood Nathan, because he didn't. For all of his charm, independence, and principles, there was a strange, moody side to his half brother that unsettled Josh. After what had just happened, he felt something more than unsettled.

The putrid smell of the bear's insides grew stronger. Josh faced into the wind and took a deep breath. Turning back toward his dad, he said, "I know bears feed at moose kills. But what will come along and clean up the mess from a bear kill?"

His father looked up, wiping at the sweat on his forehead with the back of his sleeve. "Bears," he said grimly. "No qualms about feeding on other bears." He paused. "Male bears will eat their own cubs, given a chance."

Josh shuddered inwardly.

Within an hour they had the bear skinned, gutted, and quartered. His muscles aching, Josh strapped one quarter and shoulder of the bear to his pack, while his father took the other quarter and shoulder, along with the hide. Now, on his pack, the meat was just meat, not flesh of a living creature.

Only when he looked back at the pile of guts and the head did the image of the living, breathing bear come back to him. It was a grisly picture, made more ugly by his brother's strong reaction. Nathan would really be upset if he saw the bear reduced to this, Josh thought.

The pull of the pack strained at the muscles of Josh's back, and he had to focus intently on the trail to keep from slipping. The mile and a half back to the cabin seemed twice the distance with the heavy burden of the meat.

Josh urged himself on with thoughts of what the meat would mean to them: rich soups and thick stews, along with dried jerky to chew as they followed their winter traplines. If Nathan let go of his anger and stayed, he would at least eat none of the meat. More for us, Josh thought, with just a twinge of guilt.

Maybe—maybe they wouldn't need to stretch the bear meat through the winter. Maybe Nathan would be gone, vanished from their lives, as suddenly as they had found him. And his father would realize this wilderness thing was just a crazy dream that was slowly turning to a nightmare in which they struggled at every turn for water, for food, for warmth in the winter. With Nathan gone, maybe they could go back to hamburgers and hot dogs, movies and malls, paved roads and telephones, TV and school. Funny, Josh thought. He even missed school.

Maybe they could go back to Anchorage. Anchorage had been good, the best place they'd lived since they'd wandered west from Chicago. They'd spent two years there, longer than they'd spent anywhere else. His father had found work, not great work, but steady. There Josh had friends—and he had hockey.

Josh stopped himself. If there was one thing he'd learned, it was not to hope for a change before it happened. And his little dream today hinged on his brother's foolish threat to strike out on his own in the wilderness. Josh let the twinge of guilt take root and grow to its proper size. No one should try to make it on his own in the wilderness, least of all Nathan.

3

*J*OSH'S FATHER reached the cabin first, with Josh right behind him. He gave the timbered door a shove with his shoulder, and it swung into the familiar room. The pale light of late afternoon filtered through the doorway and two small windows, illuminating the tattered sofa and lumpy armchair they had hauled from Goodwill, the table and three chairs they'd hewn from logs and branches. There was no sign of Nathan.

"Nathan?" his father called out, his eyes on the loft above.

No answer. Josh let the pack drop from his aching shoulders. "He'll be back," Josh said. He tried to sound hopeful, expectant.

Josh's father let go of his pack and stood still, watching, as if Nathan were an animal they were trying to lure from its den.

"I'll put on the coffee, Dad. Then we'll get that meat in the cellar."

"You don't think he's . . . ?"

"I think he's fine," Josh interrupted. "He's a big

17

boy, Dad. He can take care of himself. And he'll be back before dark. You'll see."

But when darkness came, Nathan still hadn't shown up. Josh had fried the bear meat, serving it with gravy over rice, and they had cached the rest of the meat in their makeshift cellar. Now they sat fighting the sluggishness that sets in after a hearty meal.

Josh held a match to the mantle of the hissing lantern, and with a pop of white light, it lit. He adjusted the valve and stared into the glow. His father sat in the easy chair, his own eyes fixed on the window and the darkness beyond.

"He's probably just trying to, well, punish us or something, Dad. For shooting the bear, I mean. It's not like he could really go anywhere. There's noplace to go."

Josh's father sighed. "Mighty cold to be sleeping outdoors."

Josh pictured his brother, shivering beside a campfire, determined not to join them in the warmth of the cabin.

"Look, I'll bet all of his stuff is still here. You want me to look?" Josh forced the words to sound casual. They should have done it when they first got home— looked to see what was missing, to see if Nathan had packed up with the intent of leaving for good.

His father shrugged his reply. The lantern light made shadows of the lines across his forehead, and his cheeks, so ruddy when he chopped ice or hauled wood, were ashen. Gray streaked the black of his beard.

Living at Willow Creek and dealing with Nathan were taking their toll. Here they sat, wondering if Nathan would come through the door at any moment, stomping his boots and warming his hands over the woodstove, giving no explanation for the time he had been missing, and no explanation demanded. That would be the way with Nathan.

But despite all Nathan's prior disagreements and disappointments with things his father and Josh said or did, he had never before threatened to go off on his own. Josh climbed the ladder to the loft. He knelt on the rough planks warmed by the rising heat and, in the dim light, surveyed the few belongings he and Nathan kept there.

In one corner sat his own wooden crate, filled with reminders of happier days. Some nights he would lie on the camp mattress beside the crate and pull out its contents one item at a time, turning each over and over in his hands, remembering back to when he'd lived much like his friends, surrounded by the lights and action of the city. He'd felt part of something then, something bigger than himself, his dad, and his brother.

There was the puck he'd shot to score the winning goal for his team in the playoffs; the note from Jenny

Hodges that he'd found stuffed inside his seventh-grade math book, the one that said how she loved looking into his deep green eyes. And, shoved down at the bottom of the crate, there was the framed photo of Josh on his mother's lap, his father's arm swung casually, happily over her shoulder. They were memories, it seemed, from another lifetime.

Josh let his eyes move to Nathan's corner of the loft, to find what he both dreaded and hoped. There was Nathan's mattress, their father's wool blanket tucked tight around the corners, in contrast to the jumble of blanket and sheets on Josh's bed. But the full-sized pack he kept propped in the corner was missing, as was the tidy stack of jeans and T-shirts that had graced the floor beside the mattress.

Josh made his way down the ladder, reaching with one foot and then the other. At the bottom, he turned and faced his father, who looked at him expectantly.

"Your blanket is still on the bed," Josh began. "But his pack and clothes are gone."

His father shook his head. "Just like Nathan. Too proud to take a blanket, even if it means he'd freeze to death."

He stood and went to the window, his face nearly pressing against the pane. "Where could he have gone?"

Josh stood next to his father. "Not far. And he could come back at any time."

"If only he'd told us sooner how he felt about that bear. He's normally so good about saying what he feels."

Josh didn't figure this was the time to disagree, but his father seemed stuck on Nathan the way he'd been when they first met up with him, when he was full of enthusiasm about moving to the woods and building a cabin so he could live in harmony with nature, so he could prove himself. But the leaner, tougher Nathan they lived with now was more withdrawn. Josh suspected there was much he kept from him and his father, both of whom failed to meet his high standards for wilderness living.

"He could survive a night or two outdoors," Josh said. "It's October, after all, not the dead of winter."

"You think he might just be making a point? Think he'll come home before long?"

"Most likely, Dad. And if he doesn't . . ."

"If he doesn't, we'll have to go looking for him. Talk him back to his senses. We need to stick together through the winter."

Josh took a deep breath.

"Dad, do you think, when we find him, when he comes home, we could talk about doing something different for the winter? Going back to Anchorage, maybe?" He tried to sound casual, not too hopeful.

"Why would we want to do that? Got a cache full of bear meat and a snug little cabin." Josh's father shook his head. "You know how Nathan hated Anchorage. Too many people. Just the idea of it would get him all riled up again."

Josh felt his hopes sink like lead. It was always what Nathan wanted. Couldn't get him all riled up. I should try getting all riled up myself, he thought. Don't I deserve a life, too? But the protests stayed locked inside Josh's head.

Suddenly his father turned from the window, his face brightening. "I'll bet he's not sleeping in the cold. I'll bet he made it over to Harry's place."

"Maybe so, Dad." Josh looked away, hiding his disappointment at the thought. He hadn't let himself think of the possibility until his father spoke the words. Nathan could hole up at Harry's indefinitely. Harry had helped them from the start, sharing all he had learned from years on a remote mining claim. Putting up a cabin at Willow Creek, near the end of the road, had been Harry's way of moving closer to civilization.

But now Harry was in Anchorage, too crippled by arthritis to care if someone moved into his place. Nathan could probably live permanently in the half-finished cabin.

Permanently. If Nathan had moved himself to Harry's cabin, they might not have to deal with him every day, but his father still would be hard-pressed to leave his older son alone in the woods. He'd want to hang around, keep an eye on him, try to smooth things over.

"We'll go there in the morning," his father said, his voice upbeat and cheerful. "Not to bother him, of course. Just to make sure that he's there. But I'm sure he is. I'd put money on it."

As if they had money to put anywhere, Josh thought. It was amazing how quickly his father's mood changed once he figured that Nathan probably wasn't far away after all.

"Let's get after those dishes before we turn in for the night," his father suggested. He set the kettle, brimming with water, atop the woodstove. Josh knelt beside the stove and stoked the fire with an armful of wood, then poked at the embers until the flickers grew to hot flames.

Closing the stove door, he leaned back and ran his hands over his shoulders and biceps, rubbing at the soreness, feeling the bulging muscles through his flannel shirt. Every fifteen-year-old boy's dream, these muscles were. Girls would have loved them, were there any girls around. His hockey coach, always harping on the boys to train in the off-season, would have been pleased. But on the frozen ponds and creeks this winter, there would be no rinks, no lights, no coach, no team.

Josh stood and stretched his legs. They had grown so long and he so tall. Those legs could probably skate faster than ever now. He closed his eyes and remembered the wind on his face, the blur of the puck at the end of his stick, the power and speed of his stride, the joy of a high shot swooshed past the goalie's outstretched glove into the corner of the net.

Opening his eyes, Josh brought himself back to reality. His skates probably didn't fit anymore. And if by some miracle he made it back to the city, he'd be so far behind the guys who'd been playing the last two seasons that he wouldn't make even a B team. Not to mention the problem of money for ice time.

While they waited for the water to boil, Josh sat at the table and pulled out an algebra lesson from the correspondence school materials stacked there. The letters, numbers, and signs of the equations looked even more confusing than they had when he'd struggled over them that morning. That morning seemed a distant memory, given all that had happened with Nathan and the bear.

Josh sighed. Taking his eighth-grade requirements by correspondence had been almost fun, as school went. He could study when and where he wanted, with no teacher harping about paying attention and getting the homework done on time.

But the high school courses seemed much more difficult, especially algebra. His father had looked over the work but couldn't remember much about these equations, and Nathan had an aversion to math.

A teacher standing over his shoulder would be welcome, much as he hated to admit it.

"I'll wash," he said, shoving the lesson back in the pile. His father, intent on a book, nodded. The tension in his face had relaxed.

"They can drip dry," Josh added. "You stay put. I wasn't getting anywhere with that algebra anyhow."

The steaming water, mixed with a splash of cold water dipped from the bucket in the corner, felt good on Josh's hands. Washing dishes without running water was one of the easier tasks they faced in their daily struggle to get by at Willow Creek. Washing jeans by hand was ten times harder.

As he scrubbed at the frying pan, Josh looked up and out the window at a star that hung far above in the lonely night. A hundred miles away in Anchorage, his friends could look up from the rink and see that star. Thousands of miles away, not far from Chicago, where his mother lived with her new husband, she could look up and see that star. Did she ever look up into the night sky and think of him?

Tonight, like most nights, Josh felt as lonely as that distant star. He wiped the last plate and set it aside to dry. The weariness of the long day settled in, and he wanted only to crawl under his covers and fade into a dreamless sleep.

4

IT ALL CAME TO PASS as Josh had suspected. Nathan settled into Harry's cabin. He received his father and brother as occasional visitors, seeming pleased with his newfound solitude. He even consented to keeping the rice and berries that their father insisted were part of his share of the food.

None of them ever mentioned the bear. Their father would carefully steer their conversations to subjects where Nathan was most comfortable—the beauty of last night's aurora, the chickadee perched on the porch railing, the tattered volume of Thoreau's *Walden* that Nathan was rereading.

Nathan could talk for a long time about Thoreau. Josh heard a lot about the naturalist, about his experiment of living alone for nearly two years at Walden Pond in a cabin he built himself.

Even though Nathan now lived in a ready-made, unfinished cabin that belonged to Harry Donaldson, he still treated it with the kind of respect that he said Thoreau extended to even the simplest aspects of life. Josh had to admit that Harry probably wouldn't object to the tidy corner of the cabin Nathan kept with the kind of reverence you might find around the altar of a country church. The dishes were always clean and the bunk always made.

Perhaps Nathan felt some ownership in the place since he had lent Harry a hand with scribing and fitting the logs during their first summer at Willow Creek. In fact, he had charmed the old man much as he had their father. Harry used to slap Nathan on the back and call him Son.

Seeing Nathan so at ease in Harry's cabin seemed to renew their father's commitment to sticking it out at Willow Creek. The state's Permanent Fund Dividend Program, which distributed a percentage of the interest earned on oil revenues to Alaskan residents, bolstered their dwindling supply of money. When the dividend checks showed up in their post office box at the end of October, Josh and his father drove into town to cash them and stock up on supplies for the winter. They would buy what they could, setting aside a bit for gasoline and emergencies, and rely on what they could hunt, trap, and gather to supply the rest of their needs.

Before heading back to the cabin, they stopped at a fast food place on the edge of Wasilla. In between handfuls of warm, salty French fries, Josh tried once more to broach the subject of moving out of the wilderness.

"You know, Dad, Wasilla wouldn't be so bad."

"So bad for what?" his father asked, wiping the grease from his fingers.

"For living in. Couldn't be more than a few thousand people here, and you could get a job."

Josh paused, glancing at a table near the door where a group of high school students, book bags flung to the floor, sat laughing and talking. Two guys sported red-and-white school jackets, with pins lined up along the letters. Three girls flashed jewelry, wearing makeup like cover girls from a supermarket magazine. Josh looked down at his own dirty jeans and turned back to his father.

His father dipped the last two fries in ketchup. "Wasilla's all right, as towns go. But who could want more than what we've got at the cabin? It's our own, free and clear, with fresh air and clean water. And we have each other."

"I know, Dad. But back when you were my age, didn't you want to be around other kids?" Josh glanced back at the booth by the door. "Just go out, hang around with your friends?"

His father pushed the tray with its rumpled napkins toward the edge of the table. "Tell you the truth, Josh, I wanted to be in the woods more than anything else. Couldn't wait for school to get out so I could check my rabbit snares or cast for pike in the lake."

"But the thing is, you could be with friends if you wanted. You had a choice."

"Saw a lot of kids get into trouble with their so-called friends. Had a few myself that tried to drag me into some things." His father nodded at the teenagers across the room.

"Take a look over there," he continued. "Looks like one girl's got a ring through the side of her nose. Lord knows what else she's got pierced. And the boys—they'll be thinking they're hot stuff, drinking on the weekends, getting girls in trouble."

He rose to his feet, wiping his hands once more on the sides of his jeans. "I don't have to worry about you doing any of that at Willow Creek. You and Nathan are getting a good solid portion of what life's all about, and you'll both be better men for it. Nathan knows that, and you'll realize it, too, as you get older."

A fleeting thought came to Josh. What if he just told his father he was fed up with living a hundred miles from nowhere? What if he told him to go on ahead, back to the land, but that he was staying right here?

"Coming?" Josh's father asked.

"Yeah," Josh said quietly. In the end, his objections would just be idle threats. He couldn't stay here by himself, with no friends, no family, no job. He stood and shoved the greasy remnants of his meal into the trash.

But if Nathan got fed up with the wilderness, Josh

knew, his father would give in. His father had no influence over Nathan. It seemed no one did.

There was no sense pursuing the matter any further. Josh gave a final glance at the table full of high school students as he rose to leave. He tried to picture himself in their midst, but the image wouldn't come. He resigned himself to being grateful that the checks had provided food beyond the bear meat and rice.

They even had a turkey for Thanksgiving. It was a lot for just the two of them, but Josh stuffed himself happily. Nathan would have none of the wanton waste he found in the holiday, when people celebrated food just for its own sake.

"Maybe we should take some food to Nathan today," Josh's father suggested the morning after Thanksgiving. Nathan didn't like taking handouts, but he could sometimes be convinced to eat their leftovers if their father insisted they'd otherwise go to waste.

"You go on ahead, Dad. I'm thinking about looking for ptarmigan up on the ridge." Josh figured he deserved a day off from correspondence lessons, especially when a C− on the last test was all he had to show for his hours struggling with algebra.

Josh swallowed the last of his coffee and pushed his cup aside. "You know, Dad, when we first got here and you let me drink coffee with you, I thought it was the greatest thing. Now I'm not even sure that I like the stuff."

"Coffee gets you going in the morning, at least," his father said. He yawned and stretched where he sat. "Start to feeling like a bear, ready to hibernate this time of year when the nights get long."

"True enough," Josh replied. The clock ticking on the shelf above the stove said ten o'clock, but through the window the sky was still streaked with the pink and orange of the dawning day. Errant flakes of snow sifted aimlessly toward the ground.

Minutes sifted like the snow, settling into one hour and then another. Gray clouds thickened in the sky, blanketing the cabin in the semidarkness of a midwinter day. The warmth of the cabin and the diffused gray light made Josh tired. He knew that getting outside would revive him, but the simple preparations for hunting threatened to sap what little energy he had.

His father was equally lethargic. He had bagged the leftovers and set them in a cool spot by the door, then stretched out on the couch, where he snored lightly. Josh caught himself dozing in the armchair. Like an old man, he thought with disgust.

The rumble of an engine outside the door startled them. It was a sound they seldom heard at Willow Creek, except for a few times when a hunter from Anchorage was adventurous enough to turn off the highway and drive the twenty miles of dirt road filled with potholes to reach the trail, barely wide enough for a truck, that ended a few hundred yards from their cabin.

Josh pushed back his chair and stood to get a good look out the window. A bright red extended-cab pickup sat in front of the cabin, looking as out of place as a robin in winter. The doors on the passenger's and driver's sides swung open at once, and Josh watched as a man climbed down from the driver's seat. He couldn't get a good look beyond the passenger door, but it seemed as though two figures had descended there.

The knock on their door was as startling as the sound of the engine had been.

"Who in the world?" Josh's father wondered aloud, reaching for the door handle. Josh stayed at the window, not having the slightest idea what to expect.

The door swung open with a creak, revealing a tall man; a boy at his side; and behind him, a girl. The man held out his hand to Josh's father.

"Frank Donaldson," he said. "And this is my daughter, Shannon, and my son, Pete. Sorry to intrude like this. We're thinking we might be a little lost."

"Donaldson." His father's voice shook ever so slightly, but he grasped the stranger's extended hand firmly. "Al Harris. And my son Josh. Please, come in."

The three stepped inside, the girl nudging the boy forward. Josh looked them all over, hoping his father would have the presence of mind to offer them a seat.

"Quite a drive you've got yourselves here," Frank said. He took off his wire-rimmed glasses and wiped at the lenses with the end of his scarf. "That last twenty miles took us an hour at least. Glad we've got the four-wheel drive."

"And guess what we saw," piped up the boy, who stood half of his dad's height. "A fox! It ran right across the road in front of us."

Frank shook his head, grinning. "It about sent us right into the ditch. Shannon here is quite the animal lover, and she screamed 'Stop!' like we were about to hit a freight train."

Josh studied the girl. Her eyes were large and brown and soulful, giving her the look of a doe staring out from the woods. They seemed to take in everything at once—the tiny room; the meager fur-nishings; the ferns of frost spread across the windows; and finally, Josh himself. He held his gaze steady, determined not to turn away.

She pulled the red wool cap from her head, and thick brown hair cascaded down. It must reach halfway down her back, Josh guessed. She looked to be older than him, by a year or two at least.

The boy was already trying to wriggle out of his coat. His sister bent down and whispered something in his ear.

Frank shifted where he stood, little puddles forming as the snow began to melt from his boots. "We're looking for my uncle Harry's place."

Josh suspected only he could read the look of dismay that passed over his father's face. "Of course, Harry Donaldson. Harry's place." He paused. Where Nathan lives, Josh added silently.

"You know him, then?" Frank asked.

His father cleared his throat. "Sure do." He paused again. "Say, if you folks have a minute, why don't you take your coats off and set a spell. We'll put on a fresh pot of coffee. Josh and I get mighty lonesome for some company."

Frank looked puzzled. "Really, we don't mean to impose. Just a few directions—"

"Might be a bit more to it than that," Josh's father said. Not giving them time to object, he added, "Here, Josh will get your things."

Josh caught the girl's eyes again as he took her coat. It was an expensive, thermal-lined brand, with trendy zippers and pockets everywhere. It smelled fresh and new. Maybe she was one of those girls who spent her weekends swooshing through powder at ritzy ski resorts. If so, she was in for a big disappointment here. He tried to guess her age. Sixteen, maybe.

"So you're Harry's nephew. How's he getting on?" Josh's father asked. He pulled out a chair for each guest. Josh scooped water for the coffee and set the pot on the stove.

"Not so well these days," Frank replied. "Sometimes he can barely get around. We're the only family he's got now in Anchorage. He's my wife's uncle, and she thinks he should move in with us, but he'll have none of it. I guess if you know Harry, that's not such a surprise."

"He's an independent sort," Josh's father said. "I do seem to remember him mentioning some family coming to Alaska from . . . where was it?"

"Seattle. Been in Anchorage since August. Harry got to talking about the cabin, and we thought we'd have a look."

"So you're just checking up on his place for him, you and the kids?"

"Sort of. Actually, he wants us to finish it up and use it. A weekend retreat from the city. He's seen how these kids love being outdoors." He laughed a little. "Not like their mother. She likes her conveniences. Says she'll let this be my project, with the kids, till we get the place fixed up."

"And how old are you, kids?" Josh could tell that his father was stalling for time, postponing an attempt at explaining why his son had set up camp in Harry's cabin.

"I'm fourteen, almost fifteen," Shannon said, her voice soft but firm.

Only fourteen, Josh thought. He had been off with his guess of sixteen. Perhaps it was the reserved look about her, as if she was taking everything in, recording it somewhere deep inside, that made her appear older. She didn't seem at all like the giggly seventh-grade girls he remembered from the last time he'd been in school.

"And I'm nine, almost ten," Pete chimed in, swinging his legs beneath the table.

"Not till July," his sister said, smiling, reaching out to smooth his sandy-colored hair.

Frank shifted in his chair and reached for the steaming cup of coffee that Josh's father handed him. "So about Harry's place. My understanding was that it was just beyond the end of this road. We parked there and walked to a cabin. But a young man met us at the door."

"What'd he say?" Josh asked, curious.

"When I mentioned Harry's name, he went on and on about what a great guy he is. But when I asked where I could find his cabin, he didn't give a real direct answer. Started talking about how mean-ingless it was to think that anything belonged to anyone, something about how a cabin is nothing more than a collection of trees that belong only to the land."

"Dad said that guy must have some case of cabin fever," Pete interrupted, grinning.

"Pete," Shannon chided. "We don't make fun of people just because they're different."

"Anyway," Frank continued, "when I saw I wasn't getting much information from him, I decided we should head back down the road and try the left fork. That's when we came upon your place. Thought sure Harry said go to the right, but maybe I got it turned around."

Josh saw his father's eyes drop toward the floor. Then he looked up and drew in a deep breath. "No, you had it right," he said. "That's my older boy, Nathan, you met there."

Frank looked puzzled. "Harry mentioned some neighbors. But not anyone living in his cabin."

Josh's father stroked at his beard. "Nathan sort of . . . took it upon himself to move into Harry's place. Takes real good care of it. Harry always liked Nathan. Guess Nathan figured Harry wouldn't mind."

Shannon looked at Josh and then at his father. "Why doesn't Nathan live here?"

Josh waited for his father to answer. The more he'd thought about Nathan's reaction to the bear shooting, the more unusual it had seemed. He wasn't about to try to explain it to a stranger.

After a few seconds, his father answered. "Nathan did stay here till just recently. But it does seem like a cabin grows smaller in the winter. And Nathan likes his privacy."

Shannon nodded. "I understand."

"Anyway, he didn't figure Harry would mind him staying there. Better to have a place lived in than empty."

"That's what Uncle Harry said when he told us we could use his cabin, didn't he, Dad?" Pete's young voice put a special emphasis on the word *we*.

Frank turned the coffee cup around in his hands. "We hate to be the ones to kick him out, but . . ."

"Look, if you aren't in too big a hurry, why don't you let me go talk this over with Nathan, explain that Harry sent you. I'm sure he'll understand."

Josh watched as his father put on his coat and tucked the bag of Thanksgiving leftovers under one arm. Once again, he was letting Nathan's actions put them all in a difficult place. He couldn't imagine Nathan backing down and coming home. And, he realized, he couldn't imagine himself having to put up with Nathan again on a daily basis. Against his better judgment, Josh let a tiny spark of hope light inside. Maybe somewhere in this mess there would be a way out—a way out of Willow Creek for good.

5

*I*T TOOK A MOMENT for Josh to realize that he'd been left with the task of entertaining three strangers.

"You want some more coffee?" he asked, holding the pot up awkwardly. He felt Shannon's eyes on him, and a warm flush crossed his face. It must look stupid, all right, a guy his age serving coffee as if he were the maid.

"Thanks, but no," Frank replied. "Think I'll go check on the truck while we're waiting. Heard a little knocking under the hood those last few miles. Probably nothing, but it never hurts to check."

"Dad," Shannon said, "get over it with the truck. You worry about that machine like it's another child."

Frank ignored her chiding. "I guess I could've offered your dad a ride, since the truck's warmed up and all. You have much trouble with keeping yours going in the winter?"

Josh smiled. "It's twenty years old, but it does all right, except when it gets real cold."

"How cold is real cold?" Frank asked.

"Oh, twenty, thirty below. Oil runs pretty thick at those temperatures."

Pete gave an exaggerated shiver. "Brrr! That's cold. Think it'll get that cold tonight?"

Josh glanced out the window at the thermometer attached to the frame near the top of the glass. Snow now fell in a thick curtain of white. "Ten degrees, and snow. I'd say you'll have to come back some other time if you want to get really cold."

The door creaked as Frank let himself out. An engine roared outside.

"Wow, that's a loud truck," Pete exclaimed.

Josh grinned. "It's not Dad's truck—it's the snow machine. Lots easier to use in the winter than a truck, and more fun to drive."

Pete stood suddenly, nearly knocking over his chair, and came to stand near Josh, where he tried to rub the frost from a bottom pane so he could see.

Josh crouched beside him and blew on the pane. He rubbed it with the sleeve of his flannel shirt, but only in time for Pete to catch a glimpse of the back of the machine as Josh's father roared off toward Harry's place.

"Maybe when he gets back, I can take you for a spin," Josh offered.

"Would you?" Pete asked, turning to look Josh in the eye. His voice sounded as if Josh had just suggested a day at the video arcade.

Shannon shook her head. "Pete, I don't know why

you find machines so appealing. They're noisy and they ruin the quiet of nature. Can't you just enjoy the outdoors on its own terms?"

Josh stood back up, turning his full attention toward the girl. "If you end up spending much time out here, you'll find the outdoors gets to be just more of the same day after day. Personally, I could do with a few more machines. They make life a lot easier and a lot more fun."

Shannon tossed her hair so that it hung neatly down her back. "Too few people realize how machines complicate our lives. We become slaves to their demands, and they pollute the environment."

Josh's mouth formed a half smile. "If having a TV and a phone makes me a slave, bring on the chains. Pretty easy to talk about doing without conveniences when you take them for granted every day. Sure, it's great getting up without an alarm buzzing in your ear. But it's all downhill from there: no hot water for a shower, no radio to give you the latest news and songs, no blow-dryer for your pretty hair."

The last part came out before Josh realized it. He hadn't meant to sound bitter and he hadn't meant to get personal. But if Shannon was offended, her face didn't show it.

"I just think we all have a lot to learn about living more simply. Have you ever read Thoreau?"

"Thoreau? The nature guy? How do you know about him?"

"My honors English class. He's my favorite author. That's why I jumped at the chance to come out here with my dad. I'd love to live in the woods like Thoreau did, away from all the commotion of the city."

Thoreau. Nathan's hero. Josh shook his head. "Once you try living in the woods, you'll find it's a lot different than you think." He turned his attention to the bear roast his father had set out to thaw by the stove. He poked at it with one finger and felt the flesh give. It was ready for the oven.

Pete was at his side. "What's that?" he asked.

Josh held the pan down so the boy could see. "Bear meat. You want some?" he teased.

Pete made a face. "Not till it's cooked. And I'm hungry right now."

"Pete, where are your manners? You don't just go around begging for food," Shannon admonished.

Josh laughed. "It's OK. I'm getting hungry myself. Not a big selection here, though."

He rummaged through the cupboard. "Here's some granola. Do you like that?"

"Does it have any chocolate pieces in it?" Pete asked.

Josh held up the clear plastic bag to scrutinize its contents. "Used to have. Those are my favorites, too.

But it looks like I left you a few." He set the bag on the table and peered deeper into the cupboard.

"Got a little moose jerky, too. Want to try some of that?"

Pete nodded eagerly. "Real moose? Did you shoot it yourself?"

"Pete, really. All these morbid details," Shannon said.

"Actually, my dad did. But I helped him cut it up and make the jerky."

"How'd you do that?"

Josh pulled out a chair for Pete and sat down beside him. "Well, you start with a couple of really sharp knives."

Shannon gave him a disgusted look and got up from the table. "If you two are going to discuss butchering, I think I'll move, if you don't mind."

"Be my guest," Josh said, making little effort to contain his grin. "You'll find out just how small this cabin really is. Can't get away from much of anything."

The glare from Shannon's eyes deepened as she moved to the couch.

"Anyway, you cut the moose in quarters," Josh continued, chewing on a handful of granola.

"What about the guts?" Pete asked.

"Oh, you gut it before you bring it home. It'd smell awful otherwise."

Pete wrinkled his nose and grabbed for another handful of granola.

"What's it taste like?" he asked, nodding toward the strips of jerky.

"Pretty much like the stuff you buy at the store. It's tough and chewy and smoke-flavored."

"I'll try some, then," Pete said, reaching for a piece. He pulled off a section with his teeth and chewed vigorously. "Not bad," he said through his mouthful.

"Glad you like it. Takes a bunch of time to slice it thin, dry it, and smoke it." Josh looked over at Shannon, sitting cross-legged on the sofa, thumbing through one of the old magazines they kept lying around. "Want to try a piece, Shannon?" he asked.

She glanced up, but Pete answered for her. "Shannon doesn't eat meat."

"Oh," Josh said. "Sorry."

"Nothing to be sorry about," Shannon replied curtly. She set down the magazine. "Do you have anything to read around here besides hunting and trapping magazines?"

Josh pulled at a piece of the jerky. The smoky flavor spread across his tongue. "No *Better Homes and Gardens,* if that's what you mean."

Shannon shot him a look. The door let in a blast of cold air as her father stepped inside. "Might be above zero out there, but the wind's picking up. Cold enough for me," he said. He stomped his feet and brushed a layer of fresh snow from his jacket.

"Maybe it's a blizzard!" Pete exclaimed.

"Don't get too excited about that idea," his father warned. "Looks like the truck's doing fine, but I don't know how much snow it could get through and still stay on that trail. Who plows around here, anyhow?" he asked Josh.

"State comes through, believe it or not. But we're low priority, after the highway. Usually have to wait a couple of days after every snowstorm."

"How much snow do you folks get?"

Josh shrugged. "Depends. Last year it was around six feet. The year before that, we heard it was ten."

"Ten feet of snow. Wow! You could build some great forts," Pete said.

"Sure could," Josh said with a smile. "We don't do much playing in it, though, except on that big bad snow machine."

"Dad, Josh said he'd take me for a ride on the snow machine when his dad gets back," Pete said.

"He said he *might* take you for a ride. We've got to get over to our own cabin—I mean Uncle Harry's—before long," Shannon said.

That all depends on Nathan, Josh thought. He wondered how his dad was doing. It wouldn't be easy, convincing Nathan he'd have to swallow his pride and move back in with them. And Josh didn't look forward to that prospect any more than he imagined Nathan did. He wished he'd been able to talk to his father before he'd left. He would have suggested they offer to leave this cabin and turn it over to Nathan. Even though they'd all built it together, it had been his brother's idea to live out here in the first place.

Then he and his father could move to Wasilla, which would be close enough to Nathan. They could live a normal life there, and his father could come out once in a while to check on Nathan if he had to. It was a great plan. Even his father would have to admit that it was in Nathan's best interests.

But he hadn't thought it through earlier, and now his father was dealing with Nathan on his own. Josh looked restlessly out the window.

Ptarmigan hunting was out of the question as long as his father had the snow machine. Besides, daylight was waning. Pete and his dad sat on the sofa, joining Shannon, who continued paging through magazines despite the fact that they weren't to her liking. With a sigh, Josh pulled out his algebra.

This new lesson on quadratic equations was even more confusing than the polynomials he had tackled with minimal success in the previous assignment. He scribbled equation after equation, erasing with more vigor each time the letters and numbers refused to find their right positions on the page.

In the middle of his frustration, Josh sensed a presence behind him. He looked over his shoulder to see Shannon standing there.

"I can help you with those if you like," she said softly.

"I just about have it." Josh almost growled the words.

Shannon ignored the tone of his voice and pulled up a chair alongside him, so close that Josh could smell the faint, clean scent of soap. His mind left the math problems and scrambled to remember when he had last bothered with a sponge bath.

"My teacher showed me an easy way to do these," she continued. "Here. Let me show you." She reached for the pencil.

Instinctively he pulled the pencil toward himself, as if he were a child with a piece of candy that he wasn't about to share. The odd look on her face made him think twice and, reluctantly, he handed over the pencil.

She copied the equation on a clean section of his paper. "Now, look," she said. "The a plus b goes here, on top."

"OK, I get it," Josh said quickly.

Shannon looked up with a smile. "Wait a minute. I'm not done yet." She scribbled more a's and b's across the page.

"See how much easier that is?" she asked. Her eyes met Josh's, and he looked quickly back at the paper.

"Yeah, but I think I'd better do it the way they show it in the book," he said.

"Nonsense. You try the next one. But do it my way."

Josh really didn't get her way. She'd gone over it too fast, a blur of scribbling on the page. And he didn't like the insistence in her voice.

He was saved from responding by the sound of the snow machine approaching the cabin. All four of them looked up expectantly, watching the door as Josh's father pushed it open.

He stood for a moment, stomping the snow from his boots, shaking it from his hat. Little icicles dripped from his beard, and his cheeks were red from the wind.

"Got a storm brewing out there," he said. Josh recognized the too-cheerful sound of his father's voice. All was not well.

6

IT TOOK A WHILE for Josh's father to get around to explaining the details of his talk with Nathan. It was over several cups of coffee, while the smell of baking bear roast filled the cabin, that he worked his way to the point.

Josh decided that Frank Donaldson had the patience of a saint. His father seemed intent on giving some—not all—of the details of his separation from Nathan and their eventual reunion in Anchorage, as if this background would help to justify Nathan's erratic behavior. Josh wished he'd just get to the heart of the matter. It was embarrassing, listening to his father recount the sorry chain of events that had brought them to Nathan and to Willow Creek.

"I can't excuse the fact that I wasn't a father to him when he needed one, while he was growing up," his father explained. "His mother and I were so young, and at that age, I couldn't imagine being tied to a wife and child. I went east and she went west with the baby, and I lost touch with them for many years."

Josh's father looked down at the floor, rubbing his boot in a small circle as if to rub out the knot in the wood beneath. "I'm not proud to say that my second marriage didn't work out so well, either. That's when Josh and I went on the road, and I took up looking for Nathan. Felt like I needed to set things right, I guess."

Josh squirmed in his seat, pretending to work through another algebra problem. Shannon, distracted by his father's story, was at least leaving him alone. But what she was hearing was no less embarrassing than her seeing that he just couldn't get quadratic equations. Would she be wondering about Josh's mother, about how she so easily let go of her only son so she could start a new life? Josh hated when people asked about his mother.

A silence fell over the cabin. Even Pete, intently drawing monster trucks on the notebook paper Josh had given him, had nothing to say. The roast sizzled and popped in the oven. The gray light from the windows, filtered through the curtain of falling snow, was fading. Before long the lanterns would need to be lit.

"And you did find Nathan," Frank prodded gently.

"Took a long time. It's a mighty big country to go looking for a person. Caught up with his mother in Billings, Montana, but by that time Nathan had already struck out on his own. Smart boy, she told me, always reading, but he had no patience with school. Left home with the clothes on his back and a hundred dollars in his pocket, headed north to Alaska. Only seventeen years old. Said he wanted to prove himself in the wilderness."

Josh remembered Billings. It was a nice town, and the school was almost brand new. Best of all, the kids didn't ask many questions. He could have been happy there for a long time, but it took only a month for his father to track down Nathan's mother, who worked days as a cashier in a local discount store and nights tending bar. As soon as his father had heard that Nathan had struck out on his own, they took off again, traveling north.

Shannon's voice interrupted his memories. "How'd he make it all the way up here with just a hundred dollars?" she asked Josh's father. Josh thought he detected a hint of admiration in her voice.

"Hitchhiked," he answered. "And worked along the way. Nathan's not afraid to work for a living." His father had a way of making everything Nathan did or said sound special, even if it was something as simple as washing dishes in a restaurant to get money to eat, which is what he was doing when they found him in Anchorage.

"That's how Nathan is," his father continued. "Proud. Independent. He won't back down from his convictions."

Frank evidently saw the opportunity to bring Josh's father to the point. "Is staying in Uncle Harry's cabin one of his convictions, then? He won't back down?"

Josh's father cleared his throat. "No, not exactly. He understands that you certainly have a greater right to be there than he does. But he'd like to believe that Harry wouldn't mind him staying there between-times, when you folks are off doing whatever you do in Anchorage."

Josh felt his dream of living a normal life in Wasilla slipping away.

A smile crossed Frank's face. "Well, that's a relief. I'll talk it over with Harry when we get back, but my guess is Nathan's right. You've been around Harry enough to know that he's an easygoing, practical sort of guy. If, as you say, he likes Nathan, it shouldn't be a problem."

Harry had always let it be known that he liked Nathan and his independent spirit. Josh's hopes deflated at the thought.

"So where will Nathan stay when we're at Willow Creek?" Shannon asked.

"Well, I must admit he was elusive on that point," Josh's father said. "Says he wants to live alone—he won't come back here. Says he's got a place in mind, but he needs to check it out first."

Josh's father cleared his throat. "So he was hoping

that maybe you folks, if you were planning to stay overnight, could hole up with us this once, just so he can be sure of his other arrangements."

"But what could those be?" Shannon persisted. "Are there other cabins out here?"

Josh's father shrugged, but Josh heard the worry in his reply. "Could be. Nathan's done plenty of back-woods hiking. Maybe stumbled on an old mining shack that he's kept to himself."

That would be typical of Nathan, Josh thought. He enjoyed withholding information, keeping secrets.

"But if you—and Harry—are willing to go along with him on this, I'd be much obliged," Josh's father said. "Keeps him close by most of the time and keeps him independent, the way Nathan likes it."

The way Nathan likes it. That was the way things always had to be. Josh felt annoyed that Frank agreed so readily to the plan his father proposed, right down to his family staying the night in this cabin instead of in the one that was rightfully theirs. All of them would be inconvenienced for Nathan's sake.

Pete got up and stood as his father's side. "Dad, where's the bathroom?" he asked quietly.

Frank grinned. "Probably right out back, just over the snowbank."

"Really?" Pete asked.

"Really. An outhouse. Like I told you to expect at Uncle Harry's, remember?"

Shannon pushed back her chair. "I'll walk you back there, Pete."

Pete gave her a disgusted look. "I can do it myself."

Shannon reached for her coat. "There's a lot of snow. I'll just make sure you find your way."

"Shannon. I'll find it."

She hesitated. "Really, it's right out back," Josh said. "Can't miss it."

Shannon relented, letting Pete go on his own, but she hovered at the window while he was out. Josh couldn't imagine that much attention aimed in one boy's direction. He wondered if their mother, the one who didn't want to spend time at the cabin till it was properly finished, was the same way.

Josh could tell by the roasted smell from the oven that their dinner was almost ready. He closed his algebra book with a slam and dug a bag of potatoes from the porch. For just about as long as he could remember, he'd been in charge of the cooking. Opening a can of soup was the extent of his father's skill in the kitchen.

He dipped a pitcher into their pail of creek water and poured it over the potatoes. One by one, he lifted them and scrubbed at the skins. Pete returned from the outhouse, and Shannon left her post by the window.

"So much snow!" Pete announced. "Maybe we could make a snowman."

"I've got a better idea," Josh said. "You come help me peel these potatoes, and I'll take you for a ride on the snow machine after dinner."

"Great," Pete agreed. He shed his coat and stood beside Josh.

"He really isn't used to handling knives," Shannon warned.

"That's OK. Josh'll show me how," Pete said, grinning. He grabbed a knife from the counter.

"Pete, put that down," Shannon scolded. "It's way too sharp for you." She stepped toward him, reaching for the handle, and Pete's grin faded. He dropped the knife with a clatter.

"See what I mean?" Shannon said, picking up the offending utensil, holding it away from her body as if it might rear up and bite someone. "That could have sliced your foot when you dropped it." She turned to Josh. "Where's the sink?"

Josh couldn't suppress a grin. "There isn't one." Her cool reserve was cracking, he realized, as he watched her expression change from concern to irritation. Her doe eyes danced with anger. She thinks I'm mocking her, he guessed.

Josh took the knife back and brought it to the dishpan, where he dipped it in the sudsy water they kept on hand, then rinsed it with a splash of steaming water from the kettle on the stove. He wiped the blade dry and returned to Pete's side.

"This knife's probably too dull anyway," Josh said. "You can use the peeler instead."

Pete's grin returned, and they set to work, with Shannon hovering beside Pete, her eyes never leaving his fingers.

"I can help if you like," Shannon offered.

Josh shrugged. "Sure. Dump that bag of cranberries into a saucepan. They should be thawed by now."

"They are," Shannon said as she followed his directions. Josh set the potatoes to boil in water and dumped sugar in with the cranberries. He handed Shannon a wooden spoon.

"Now stir," he instructed. He pulled the roast from the oven of the wood stove and set it on the carving board.

"It's starting to boil," Shannon said, peering into the saucepan.

"Good. Keep stirring till it gets thick. Pete, you'd better watch her to make sure she's doing it right."

Pete obediently left Josh's side and stood by his sister. Shannon glared at Josh, but he pretended not to notice.

"Sure is nice to have dinner prepared for us," Frank said when they all sat at last around the table. Josh felt strangely lower than the others. He sat on the footstool pulled over from the easy chair, and his father sat tall, perched on a stepladder.

Josh ladled the cranberries alongside a thick slice

of meat. He had picked them one by one in September, on a clear, bright afternoon following the first frost. He scooped a bit of the sauce onto his fork and brought the tangy taste to his lips, letting it spread through his mouth like the memory of September sunshine.

"I thought cranberry sauce only came out of cans," Pete said as he scooped a generous portion onto his plate.

"So who shot the bear?" Frank asked.

"Josh did," his father replied. "Got us out of a mighty sticky situation in the process."

"And what was that?" Frank asked between bites.

Josh's father swallowed. "Found it on a moose kill. We were trying to figure the best shot when it charged." Josh wasn't surprised that his father left out the part about Nathan's wild, irrational reaction, knocking the gun from his father's hands, putting all of their lives at risk.

Pete turned to Josh. "You killed a *charging* bear? I want to go hunting with you sometime."

Josh grinned. "Hunting season's over, for big animals anyhow. Now I just go after ptarmigan and rabbit. We mostly trap in the winter, while the furs are good."

Pete licked a bit of cranberry sauce from his fingers. "Maybe I could go trapping with you, then."

"Sure," Josh replied. "You could come along." He

noted Shannon's glare of disapproval. "Sometime," he added.

The glare continued. "Pete," she said in a low voice.

"Aw, Shannon. My friend Bobby's dad says the animals don't suffer."

"Don't suffer?" she said indignantly, her voice a low hiss. "Caught in the jaws of a trap and left to die, slowly and painfully? Of course they suffer."

Josh stabbed at a large piece of tender meat. "That's not how it is. We only use traps and snares that, when set properly, kill quickly and efficiently."

Shannon's eyes flashed defiantly. "Quickly and efficiently. Like a guillotine." Her voice was louder now, and Josh saw Frank shoot a glance in their direction.

He kept his voice calm. "That's not the best of comparisons. Maybe a guillotine is quick and efficient, but it's used to kill people, not animals. There's a lot more room for debate there."

"Is there?" Her voice grew louder still.

"For one thing, some of these animals are destined to die a much slower, more painful death at the hands of Mother Nature, through winter starvation and cold. And man is their natural predator." Josh saw Pete nodding his head, as if in synchronization with his words.

Silence set in across the table. Trying to change to

a casual tone, as if they had been talking about the weather, Josh held the platter of meat in front of Shannon. "Care for some roast?"

"No, thank you," she said, her eyes flashing and her words pointed. "I don't eat meat."

That knife would come in handy now, Josh thought, to cut the tension around the table. He set down the platter, embarrassed that he hadn't remembered.

But his embarrassment quickly turned to irritation. She was on a high horse, just like Nathan, trying to make them feel bad for a simple thing like eating meat. He stabbed at a chunk of roast on his plate and brought it to his mouth. He chewed it for a long time, savoring the sweet, pungent taste. He wasn't about to let her make him feel guilty.

7

PETE REMINDED JOSH about the promised snow machine ride three times before the meal was over. By the time the table was cleared, he'd pulled on his snowsuit and boots and was standing at the door.

"I'm ready, Josh," he announced.

"I see that," Josh said with a smile. He reached for the insulated coveralls hanging on a peg by the door. He felt sluggish again after the meal, and he'd been cooped up inside all day. A ride would feel great.

"Don't go too fast," Shannon cautioned as they went out the door.

"Right," Josh said over his shoulder. So only Pete could hear, he added, "You don't want to go fast, do you?"

Pete look up at him earnestly. "Sure I do."

"Well, what your sister doesn't know won't hurt her, right?"

"Right," Pete agreed.

The snowstorm had gone as quickly as it had come, leaving four inches of fresh powder over everything. A snowfall made the woods seem like a brand-new creation, covering tracks left by man, animal, and machine, leaving new curves and mounds of white on every branch and bough. With the end of the storm, the temperature had predictably dropped. Josh felt the sting of cold on his nose and pulled the fleece neck warmer up to his eyes.

"Pull up your hood and tighten it," Josh instructed Pete, his voice muffled by the fleece. "If we put the helmet over the hood, it should stay on."

Pete looked like a miniature spaceman in the oversized helmet. Josh stifled a grin.

He pulled at the cord of the machine, and the sound of the engine overcame the stillness of the night. He pushed the throttle, letting the track, propped up on a block of wood, spin free of snow and ice. Thick exhaust poured from underneath, and Pete stepped back, away from the fumes.

Josh lifted the machine from the block, letting the back end drop to the ground with a thud. "Hop on!" he said loudly.

Pete settled onto the seat, with Josh in front, and they took off. Josh maneuvered slowly through the trees in front of the cabin, but once they were out of range of Shannon's watchful eyes, he pressed deeper on the throttle. Walls of spruce trees, their boughs hanging heavy with snow, closed in on either side. Traveling through them, Josh felt like a time voyager, warping his way to another world.

When they reached a clearing, Josh brought the

machine to a stop. Over the loud noise of the idle, he asked Pete, "You want to try?"

"Driving? You bet!" Even past the hood and the plastic bubble of the helmet's face shield, Josh could see his wide grin.

"OK. Not much to it, really." He climbed off the machine and pointed. "The throttle here makes it go, and this lever is the brake. The red button is the kill switch, in case you need to stop in a hurry."

Pete nodded and took off, tentatively at first and then with more force. Josh watched with a growing feeling of satisfaction, remembering the first time he'd sat behind the handlebars of the machine and sensed that he was at last in total control of something in his life.

Making a wide loop at the end of the clearing, Pete was careening back toward the spot where Josh stood waiting when the machine jerked suddenly to the right. Josh watched, horrified, as Pete lost control and went flying off the seat of the machine, landing face down in the snow. The machine lay on its side, the track still spinning.

Josh felt a horrible sinking sensation spread to the pit of his stomach as he ran and knelt next to Pete. He reached out and put a hand on his shoulder.

"Pete? You OK, buddy?"

Pete lifted his head slowly and looked around. "Wow. What happened?"

"Looked to me like you hit a bump, maybe a stump buried under the snow, and lost control. Does anything hurt?"

Pete rolled to his back and sat up before Josh could caution him otherwise. "Naw, I'm fine. That was cool. Can I try it again?"

Josh brushed the snow from Pete's suit. "I don't think so. Flying through the air like that can be hard on a person. You sure you're all right?"

Pete nodded, the weight of the helmet forcing his head to bob vigorously. "I'm sure."

Josh allowed himself to smile faintly. "Fresh snow makes a great cushion at least. And now you see why we wear helmets." He pulled Pete to his feet, and the thumping of his heart diminished. He'd flown off the machine himself before, but it had been more frightening watching Pete do it.

Josh hit the kill switch and grabbed the handlebars, pushing all his weight against the machine to set it upright.

"Listen," he said to Pete before they climbed back on. "Let's keep this part of the ride to ourselves. We wouldn't want to worry your sister."

Pete nodded in agreement and climbed on behind Josh. The ride back was a little slower and much less eventful.

As they pulled up to the cabin, a figure emerged. Josh brought the machine to a stop, turned the key, and looked up to see Shannon standing on the steps.

Pete hopped off and ran to his sister.

"How was it?" she asked, giving him a little hug.

"Great!" Pete exclaimed, pulling the helmet from his head. "You should try it."

"I'm ready," Shannon said, a look of determination in her eyes.

"Thought you didn't like machines," Josh said.

"I've decided it's an experience. I like new experiences." Her voice was firm.

Josh gave her a long look. She wasn't going to ask if he'd take her for a ride. She just expected it.

He gave the cord of the machine a jerk, feeling the irritation ripple through the muscles of his arm. "Hope you've got some long johns on under those jeans," he yelled over the engine noise. "It gets colder once we start moving."

Shannon stepped closer. "I'll be fine."

Josh shook his head. Those jeans fit like a second skin over her narrow hips and long legs. Of course she wasn't wearing an extra layer.

They took off with a roar. Josh decided he'd drive as fast as he pleased and try to forget that the arms of a girl he had only just met were wrapped around his waist. The trees sped by in an evergreen blur.

"Duck!" he yelled, and ducked himself, under a hanging branch. If she didn't do the same, she would go flying off the machine. But the arms were still there, and he felt her scoot forward, readjusting herself closer to his back.

Now they entered the meadow where the thin light of the moon and the stars was magnified by a mirror of snow. Josh pushed harder on the throttle, and they careened across the wide-open space. The machine almost floated over the smooth surface, and Josh felt a familiar exhilaration at the rushing air and the speeding scenery.

Then a thin voice reached his ears through the helmet.

"Stop! Stop!"

Josh slid the machine to a stop and hit the kill switch. He turned his head to see what was wrong.

Shannon let go of his waist and stood beside the machine. She slipped off her helmet and tipped her head backward, her eyes intent on the sky.

"What's the matter?" he asked, pulling off his own helmet.

"You were going so fast," she said, her voice hushed. "And the stars were just a blur. Look at them now. There must be thousands up there. They're fabulous!"

Josh shook his head. Fabulous. Same stars she saw in Anchorage.

Then he remembered all the times he'd looked to

the stars, seeing them as a single point of connection between himself and the people he loved, and his hard edge of resentment softened. He watched as Shannon stood, gazing from one end of the black sky to the other, as if she were memorizing the position and intensity of each glittering light.

He got off the machine and stood beside her, looking up. Almost imperceptibly, she shivered. Without thinking, Josh nearly wrapped an arm around her, drawing her toward his warmth as a father would a child. But in the next moment, he felt foolish for even allowing himself to consider it.

She most certainly would have jerked away. That's what had happened the last time he had put his arm around a girl, during the seventh-grade social back at East Anchorage Middle School.

Besides, he and Shannon were clearly cut from different molds. He wouldn't want her thinking he was making moves on her, like he was some kind of love-starved wild man of the woods.

Josh stepped back. "You must be frozen. We'd better get going," he said curtly.

Shannon climbed on the machine behind him and her arms found their place around his waist. He started the machine. Before hitting the throttle, he turned his head and said loudly, "Next time, you'll wear long johns."

"I wouldn't be so cold if you'd drive a little

slower." Josh barely heard her words as he gunned the throttle and they took off.

Josh woke the next morning to a thin, bluish light seeping past the curtains of the loft and knew immediately that he had slept too long. His limbs felt heavy and his head fuzzy. Judging by the approaching sunrise, it had to be close to 10 A.M.

He sat up, stretching his arms out in front of him, yawning and shaking the drowsiness from his head. In the winter, sleep came early and lasted long. He couldn't have been up much past eleven the night before, begging off Frank's challenge for a rematch of 500 rummy and crawling up to the loft, where Pete was already stretched out on the mattress that had been Nathan's.

Pete lay there now, his body curled like a leaf on a newly sprouted plant. Still fast asleep, he looked as young and vulnerable as one, too.

"Hey, buddy," Josh said, setting a hand on Pete's shoulder. "Rise and shine. The day will be half gone before you get out of here."

Pete rubbed at his eyes and opened them wide. "Get out of here to go where?"

"Home, remember? You guys are going home today."

"Oh, yeah." His voice was flat with disappointment.

"You'll be back before long. Christmas break, your dad said. You'll get to sleep at Harry's place then. And I'll take you trapping like we talked about. Only I wouldn't tell your sister if I were you."

Pete's face brightened. "Trapping. Cool. Don't worry, I won't tell."

"Smells like pancakes down there," Josh said. Pete was fumbling with the buttons of his flannel shirt, the lower half of his body still encased in the sleeping bag. "Last one to the outhouse gets to do dishes," Josh added.

When his feet hit the floor at the bottom of the ladder, Josh was surprised to see Shannon standing at the cookstove flipping the hotcakes. She had pulled her hair back into a long, loose ponytail, but wisps of it curled here and there around her face.

Shannon looked over her shoulder at Josh, and he smiled slightly in spite of himself. He thought he detected a hint of a smile in return, but it was hard to tell in the shadowy morning light.

He flung on coat and boots for a quick trip to the outhouse but found himself lingering on his return. There was an almost magical quality to the winter morning. Light filtered sideways through the trees, streaking the sky with cotton-candy pinks and blues. Every twig and bough was bent heavy with snow, forming a collage of arches in the woods. If he'd gotten up earlier, he might have been treated to the sound of an owl hooting its last call before bedding down for the day, but now there was only the silent hush of winter in the woods.

He had to admit there was nothing like a run to the outhouse on a cold morning to wake a person up and make him feel really alive. But then, Josh reminded himself as he stomped up the steps of the cabin, there were plenty of other things to make a person feel alive—MTV; girls; movies; hockey; even school, where you'd see more people in an hour than you'd see at Willow Creek all year.

He met Pete at the door, bundled up for his own outhouse visit.

"Brrr!" Pete said. "How cold is it out here?"

Josh breathed in deep, filling his lungs with cold air. "Colder than yesterday, I'd say. Ten below, maybe. Let's take a look."

He leaned over to check the thermometer nailed to the window frame. "A balmy eight below. Did you bring a pair of shorts?"

Pete grinned and shifted slightly. "I don't think so." He shifted again. "I gotta go," he added, pointing at the outhouse.

"Don't let me keep you," Josh said, giving him a little shove in the right direction.

Shannon handed Josh a plate of steaming hot-cakes when he got inside, and he sat and ate as though he hadn't eaten for days, savoring the warm mix of butter and syrup. Cold granola just wasn't the same. His father and Frank were huddled on the sofa, with Frank looking over a plat book that mapped borough land while Dad explained where their plot and Harry's lay.

"Good breakfast," Josh said to Shannon between bites. "Any coffee left?"

Even though he drank coffee every morning with his father, today in front of Shannon and Pete, it made him feel older, more mature.

Pete had pulled his chair right alongside Josh to eat his own plate of hotcakes.

Frank stood up from the sofa and stretched. "Finish up those last few bites, Pete. We need to get going. With fresh snow on the road, we'll have to drive slower on the way out."

Shannon leaned over Pete, peering at a pink area on the right side of his forehead, half covered by his hair. She rubbed it lightly.

"Pete, how did you get this bump?"

Pete gave Josh a knowing look and shrugged his shoulders. "I don't know," he said.

"You need to be more careful," Shannon scolded. "That's close to your temple."

"Al, much obliged for your hospitality," Frank was saying.

"Our pleasure," Josh's father responded. "Sorry

about the, uh, confusion with Nathan. He'll be out of there when you come back next month."

"You mean we won't get to talk to him again?" Shannon asked. She sounded disappointed.

"Honey, from what we've heard, Nathan's something of a free spirit. He'll talk with us on his own terms, wouldn't you say, Al?"

"That's Nathan, all right," Josh's father answered with pride.

It took a few moments for Frank, Shannon, and Pete to put on all of their gear and gather their things. Just before they went out the door, Pete sneaked back to Josh and whispered, "Remember—trapping."

Josh grinned and tousled the boy's hair. "It's a deal," he said under his breath.

He followed the sound of the truck as it faded into the distance. As he listened, he let himself imagine the life Shannon and Pete were returning to, a life like the one that he longed for himself, filled with friends and phone calls and maybe even dates.

Then the rumbling of the truck faded completely, and a stillness settled over the cabin once more.

8

Bears are made of the same dust as we, and breathe the same winds and drink of the same waters. A bear's days are warmed by the same sun, his dwellings are overdomed by the same blue sky, and his life turns and ebbs with heart-pulsings like ours and was poured from the same fountain.

JOHN MUIR

Josh READ THE QUOTE, printed in Nathan's precise capitals and tacked to the log wall above the bunk where he slept. Alongside it hung pictures of bears carefully clipped from magazines. One showed a polar bear lumbering across a sheet of ice, its clawed toes pointed inward. Another showed a grizzly, its silver-tipped fur gleaming in the sunlight, pawing a bright red salmon from a stream.

It was the photo of a black bear, standing on its hind legs, its dark eyes staring into the camera, that most struck Josh, bringing to mind the day when Nathan had seemed so willing to sacrifice all of their lives out of devotion to a bear. Josh's eyes dropped to the shelf beside the bunk. He saw a crude drawing, done in ink, of two black bears, paws lifted toward each other, whether in play or in battle, Josh couldn't tell.

He looked back at the quote, trying to piece it together with the photos and the drawing. *His life turns and ebbs with heart-pulsings like ours and was poured from the same fountain.* The words suggested a mystical connection with the animal. Josh couldn't relate.

He felt Nathan's eyes on him, staring. "Who's John Muir?" Josh asked lightly.

Nathan sniffed at the pot of soup he stirred and looked up. "A naturalist. He explored the wilds of America at the end of the nineteenth century. There's a glacier named after him." Nathan paused to bring a spoonful of broth to his lips. He blew on it, then slurped a taste.

"Just right," he proclaimed. He smiled, pleased with his efforts. "Let's eat."

Josh pulled up a chair beside his father at the table. He still felt like an intruder whenever they visited Nathan in Harry's cabin. It didn't matter that Frank had sent a note confirming that Harry would allow Nathan to stay, as long as he was willing to make other arrangements whenever the Donaldsons came back.

Frank had even included a list of the upcoming holiday weekends when he and the kids had tentative plans to visit the cabin and do a little finishing work to get it up to what he called "the wife's standards." The first of those weekends began the next day, but

Nathan seemed unconcerned. In fact, he seemed downright cheery.

"Great soup," his father said.

Josh brought a spoonful of the watery broth to his lips. A few grains of rice floated among bits of canned carrots and beans. He let the flavor settle on his tongue before he swallowed. It was on the bland side, but it brought a welcome warmth. Nathan kept his cabin chilly.

"You like it, Josh?" Nathan asked.

"Sure."

"You two can take the leftover soup if you like. I won't be needing it."

Josh watched his father's eyes fill with concern. "Nathan, you make it sound like you're going away forever. I wish you'd tell us where you'll be."

Nathan shook his head resolutely. "I've got to work it out on my own."

"But it would be so easy for you to just move in with us while the Donaldsons are here. Josh and I would stay out of your way, wouldn't we, Josh?"

Josh nodded, though he wasn't clear how you stayed out of anybody's way in a 10 x 20 cabin. Spend a lot of time on the trapline, he supposed. If the weather continued to be as mild at it had been, up into the twenties for the last few days, that would be easy enough.

"Dad," Nathan said. "I know you mean well. But

being on my own here turned out to be for the best. I never should have spent all that time living with you two in the first place. What I always wanted was to prove myself in the wilderness, on my own."

Josh watched for his father's reaction. His eyes looked puzzled, but he kept listening.

"Now this is a greater opportunity for me to prove to myself that I can survive alone, even in the dead of winter."

Their father stroked at his beard. "Dead is what you'll be if you're not careful. The arctic cold is no man's friend."

Nathan nodded. "I know it'll be tough," he acknowledged. "But I did some reading before I came up here. And I've read some in Harry's books. Think of all the indigenous peoples who've survived whole winters in primitive shelters at more extreme temperatures than these. We're just talking about a few days."

Their father raised an eyebrow. "Are you saying you're going to build yourself an igloo like the Eskimos live in up north?"

"Dad," Josh interrupted. "Nobody lives in igloos anymore, and the Eskimos in Alaska never did." He'd learned that in seventh-grade social studies.

"Josh is right," Nathan agreed. "They lived in sod huts." He stirred at the last bit of soup in his bowl. "And they stayed quite warm. You act like shelters made from natural elements like snow and earth are inferior to those that are manmade."

Their father pushed his bowl to the side and leaned forward. "All I'm saying is that you should take a few precautions, like telling us where you'll be. We'd leave you alone, but at least we could find you if . . . if something went wrong."

A hint of a smile formed above Nathan's scraggly beard. "The adventure comes with the risk."

He rose from the table and stacked their bowls beside the dishpan. Josh wondered how long it took him to haul his water on foot, bucket by bucket. The creek was a good quarter mile away. Josh found the task tedious even using a snow machine, a sled, and a forty-gallon pail.

"Good to see you," Nathan said abruptly. It was his way of dismissing them.

"So you'll be gone when the Donaldsons get here tomorrow?" Josh's father asked as he zipped his jacket.

"More or less," Nathan answered vaguely.

Even after they returned to their own cabin, Josh saw the worry that hung in his father's eyes.

Josh lit the lantern and hung it in a frosty window. A circle of light spread across the blanket of snow tucked neatly around the cabin. Beyond the solitary trail to Harry's cabin, no track of man or animal marred the thick cover, as if in the still and dark winter night, life had drained itself from the landscape. Crystalline edges of individual flakes caught the light, glinting upward toward the darkened sky, where a myriad of stars glinted back.

As a child, Josh had heard that every snowflake had a different pattern, unique from all others that had ever fallen. But surely that couldn't be true. Beyond the circle of light, the two-foot layer of snow stretched for miles into the darkness, across the meadow, over Willow Creek, and up the face of Denali, the great mountain. There the layers deepened and hardened, topping vast expanses of glacial ice that crawled into valleys. And from there the snow stretched on for hundreds of miles, north to windswept Barrow; west to the ice packs of the Bering Sea; east to the frozen depths of the Canadian Arctic; and south to Anchorage, where traffic ground it to gray slush. What was one snowflake in all of that?

He turned back toward the room. A dreary sameness hung about it, despite the scraggly spruce tree that stood propped in one corner, its boughs strung with limp strands of cranberries and popcorn. This Christmas, like the last, had been far from festive, with no lights, few gifts, and no one but his father and his brother to share it with.

His father sat motionless, bent toward a book opened across his lap. The lantern light threw dark lines across his face, and Josh could tell by the blank look in his eyes that he wasn't really reading but pondering something, most likely his older son.

Josh sat on the sofa beside his father. He leaned forward, elbows on his knees, and took a deep breath.

"Dad, you know, maybe it would be better, better for Nathan, if he could have this cabin. I mean, he wants to prove himself, living alone. It doesn't sound like he has any intention of moving back in while we're here."

"No, it doesn't." His father's voice sounded small and distant.

Josh shifted where he sat, choosing his words carefully. "Well, if he insists on living alone, wouldn't he be safer living here than out there somewhere?" He lifted his eyes toward the vast expanse of wilderness beyond the window.

His father sighed and looked at Josh with weary eyes. "He would be safer, but I'm not sure how he'd do all alone, even with a snug cabin to shelter him. Have you noticed how thin he's getting?"

"He's always been thin, Dad. Nathan has his standards about what he'll eat."

"That's just it. His standards. I hate to say this about your brother, but sometimes he lets his standards rule over good old common sense. That's where you and I come in."

"But Dad," Josh said. He struggled with the sound

of his voice, not wanting to sound urgent or pleading. "It's not as if we have to abandon Nathan. We could be nearby." He hesitated. "Wasilla, maybe. We could come out on weekends. I'll bet we could stay at Harry's place, when the Donaldsons aren't there. And when they are, they could check up on Nathan."

His father put a hand on Josh's knee. "I know you'd like that." He paused. "And who knows, maybe it would be best, for you and for Nathan. I'll have to think about it."

Josh allowed himself a little smile. It was the most cause he'd had for hope in a long time.

9

THE DOOR OPENED WIDE and Shannon greeted Josh, her eyes lively and her face flushed.

"Hi! If you came looking for your brother, he just left," she explained.

Josh looked over his shoulder, noting a line of footprints heading into the woods.

"He's an incredible person, isn't he?" Her voice was full of admiration.

"He's different," Josh admitted. "Actually, I came for Pete."

"Oh," she said. "Come in."

Pete hopped off the bunk at the sight of Josh. "Guess what I got for Christmas?" Without waiting for a reply, he continued. "A brand new pair of skates!"

Josh grinned. "That's great. You know, I used to play hockey before we moved out here."

"You did? My friend Mike plays hockey. I wanna play, too. But first I gotta learn to skate."

"That helps."

"Hey, maybe you could teach me. I'll bring my skates next time."

"Sure thing." Josh didn't want to squelch Pete's enthusiasm by telling him about the hours of shoveling they'd have to do to clear even a tiny rink on the pond. He shifted uncomfortably, aware of the growing pool of melting snow beneath his boots.

"Say, Pete, you ready for a ride?"

Pete gave him a knowing look. "Oh, yeah," he said. "I'm ready. I already told Dad you'd be taking me out."

"Out where?" Shannon asked.

"Oh, just out and about," Josh replied.

Pete hurried to pull on his snowsuit. Frank stuck his head around the corner of the cabin's only inside wall, the one that set off an area that Harry used for storage. "Hello, Josh. Good to see you again. Shannon, did we bring those three-inch nails?"

"We brought two bags of nails. Are those the ones?"

Frank shook his head. "No. I meant to bring a third." He sighed. "I guess this other set of bunks will have to wait. No running back to town from here." He paused a moment, staring back where he'd been working.

"Dad might have some three-inch nails," Josh offered. "Leftovers from when we put our place up."

"I think I'll go check on that, then. Pete, you're going trapping with Josh?"

"Dad!" Pete said. He struggled with his last mitten. "You weren't supposed to tell."

"Sorry," Frank admitted. "But I'm sure your sister won't interfere. Will you, Shannon?"

Shannon's eyes narrowed, but she kept her silence. Her father stepped around her to get his coat and hat.

"I can give you a ride over there if you want," Josh offered. "Pete can ride in the sled."

"Thanks, but the walk will do me good," Frank replied. He pulled the door shut behind him, leaving Josh to face Shannon.

Shannon drew in a deep breath and steadied herself. She spoke slowly, deliberately, her eyes fixed on Josh, her words directed at her brother. "Pete, I don't think that riding around for hours in the cold looking at dead animals is the best way for you to spend your time."

Josh took a step closer to her. He looked down into her face and spoke in a loud whisper. "And how would you suggest he spend his time here? Surfing the Internet? Watching the home shopping channel? Cruising the malls? In case you haven't noticed, we don't have any of your kind of entertainment out here."

"And who said that was my kind of entertainment?" Shannon sputtered back.

Josh ignored the question. "Trapping is one of the ways we put food on the table. It's how we get a little money to live on." Josh glanced over at Pete, who was watching them, wide-eyed. Maybe he'd never seen anyone stand up to his sister before, Josh thought. If not, it was about time he saw someone who would.

"Your brother Nathan doesn't need to kill animals to survive in the wilderness," she retorted.

"My *half* brother Nathan has some strange ideas."

"I don't think his ideas are strange. He believes in respecting the earth and all of its inhabitants."

"And how did that topic come up on his way out the door?"

"We sat and had some herbal tea with him before he left. And we just got to talking, about why he came to live here," she retorted, her voice smug.

"Let's see. I'll bet he said he wanted to prove himself in the wilderness."

"Something like that."

"And I don't suppose he mentioned how our father watches out for him every step of the way, so he doesn't starve to death or something with all of his noble ideas."

"As a matter of fact, he said he'd rather live truly on his own. He was looking forward to these few days away."

Josh remembered his father's parting words when he'd gone off with the snow machine. "See if you can figure out where your brother's headed. Maybe you can follow his tracks."

He sighed. Ever his brother's keeper. "I don't suppose he said anything about where he might be going."

"No," Shannon said, as proudly as if she herself had shown such independence. "He didn't."

Josh glanced at the bunk. All of the bear photos were still tacked to the wall, along with the quote. Nathan would be coming back, anyhow.

"Josh, I'm getting hot. Can we go now?"

"Sure thing, buddy. That is, if your sister's not going to stand in our way."

Shannon looked away for a moment. When she returned her gaze, her brown eyes flashed with defiance. "Fine," she said resolutely. "He can go. But I'm going, too."

"You'll get cold."

She was already reaching for a pair of snow pants. "No, I won't."

"You'll get sore, riding in the sled."

She pulled on her boots. "I don't care."

"You won't like what you see. Most likely some dead animals."

She zipped her coat. "I know that."

"Then why do you insist on coming?"

"If you're dragging Pete into this, the least I can do is be there. For support."

Josh let out a little laugh. "For support." He shook his head. "All right, then. Let's go."

The trail was full of bumps, and with the sled behind, Josh had to go extra slow. At the first stop, Pete climbed off the machine with Josh. His sister stayed where she sat.

"Now what?" she asked. The words snapped like a frozen branch.

"Now we check the first set," Josh replied. He reached over Shannon for his basket of traps and lures. She shifted out of his way. He felt the force of her inattention, her determination to ignore his actions.

"What's a set?" Pete asked.

Josh slung the leather straps of the basket over his shoulders. The basket hung heavy, like an awkward, oversized backpack.

"I'll show you," Josh said. "Follow me."

He trudged ahead to where a tall, straggly spruce stood above the rest of the trees, following the faint outlines of boot prints from his last visit. Several inches of snow had all but erased them. He looked back to see Pete struggling to plant his boots, one step at a time, in the larger tracks Josh was making, giving the impression that only one walked here instead of two.

When they reached the tall spruce, Josh knelt at its base and brushed the snow away from a gentle mound, revealing a three-sided formation he had fashioned of sticks braced against the trunk of the tree.

"This is a set," Josh said. "A cubby set. The trap sits at the front and the bait is inside. The animal has to step in the trap to get to the bait."

"Can I look inside?" Pete asked. He knelt in the soft snow beside Josh.

"Sure."

Pete peered into the set. "There's no animal."

"Nope. No action here."

The second set showed no sign of action either. Josh felt a familiar discouragement set in. If his father was going to seriously consider Josh's plan to give the cabin to Nathan and move to Wasilla, they'd need some money to get started. And selling furs was the only hope for that.

At the third stop, Josh brushed the snow from the entrance of the cubby set, revealing the lifeless brown form of a large marten. He sprung open the jaws of the trap and lifted the creature out of its hold so that Pete could have a closer look.

"Can I touch it?" Pete asked. The boy's eyes held the same mix of curiosity and horror that Josh remembered feeling the first time he'd seen a dead animal up close. For Josh it had been when he was a year or two younger than Pete, on his first deer hunting trip with his dad, back in Montana. One moment the buck had sprung out of the woods and into the meadow, and the next its long legs had crumpled, the graceful animal brought down by a bullet from his dad's rifle.

As many animals as Josh had seen killed since that day, often by the work of his own hands, he had never grown used to the stiff, cold reality of death, which wrung all life from a creature in one final instant. Maybe no hunter or trapper ever did.

Pete pulled off a mitten and stroked a finger along the thick, dark fur of the marten's back. "So soft," he said. "What do you do now?"

"Reset the trap, take the marten home, skin it, and sell the fur," Josh said matter-of-factly. He lifted the lid of the trapper's basket and dropped the animal inside. Then he glanced back at the sled, only twenty yards away. Shannon sat with her knees drawn up close to her chest, staring off at the horizon, acting as if she hadn't seen the dead marten or the trap that caught it, as if by sheer will she could alter this reality.

"Getting cold yet?" Josh spoke the words loudly.

Her response was a flash of her dark eyes, the only part of her face visible above the edge of her red scarf.

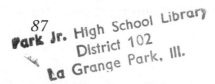

Her eyelashes and the wisps of hair around her face had grown frosty, and Josh saw that her cheeks were pale, not rosy like her brother's.

Josh knew she had to be chilled, sitting virtually motionless there on the sled for the last hour. She must be sore already, too. Josh felt a twinge of guilt. He could have lined the sled with a few sleeping bags to cushion her.

It was utter foolishness, this insistence that she ride along for Pete's benefit. She should be back in the warmth of the cabin, reading some book that let her experience nature from a distance, without the harsh realities of cold and death to deal with.

Josh reset and baited the trap, and Pete helped him arrange the pine boughs that camouflaged the set.

"You could catch another one in the same place?" Pete asked.

Josh nodded. "Once you've caught one there, you know you've got a good spot, where the animals are active."

"I thought you looked for tracks or something."

Josh shrugged. "Sometimes. But tracks can be hard to follow." Even human tracks, Nathan's tracks. He'd made a brief attempt to locate his brother at the beginning of their expedition, following alongside Nathan's meandering footprints for a while. Where the tracks plunged into a ravine, Josh had slowed the machine and squinted, trying to make out where they led so he could pick up the trail on the other side. But he lost sight of them, and when he drove around to the upper edge, he didn't see where they came out, either. At least he could tell his father he'd tried.

"Climb back on the machine, buddy. Next stop's the creek."

Pete scrambled onto the seat. Josh glanced at Shannon and said, "That's where you get out and get your blood moving."

Shannon did climb out of the sled when they reached the creek. She followed as Josh and Pete picked their way along the frozen bank.

Josh turned to Pete. "Here we'll look for tracks."

Pete looked puzzled, so Josh explained. "Mink like to travel along the frozen creek. With this new snow, we should see some fresh tracks to tell us where to hang the snares."

They tromped on, their boots crunching and squeaking against the dry snow. The sky above them was the palest of blues, lit only by an angle of light. All around, the snow seemed tinged in blue as well. Josh found his eyes seeking out other shades—the purer white of birch bark, the grayish trunk of a cottonwood, the dark branches of the spruce heavy with their burden of snow. Then, through the trees, he spotted a patch of gray-white, not more than fifteen yards away.

Josh stopped abruptly, putting a hand out behind him to alert Pete.

"What?" Pete began.

"Shhh!" Josh kept his eyes focused on the patch of gray and white. He could barely detect the texture of fur through the trees.

The creature stepped past the cover of the trees and stood as still as they. Then Josh saw the wary fleck of the tail, and the head turned to look them full in the face. Josh hoped Pete and Shannon would stay still.

The green eyes seemed to freeze them in time. The whiskers twitched and the ears, spiked with longish hair, quivered ever so slightly. Josh hoped that Pete could see it as well as he could.

Suddenly the animal bounded away from them, its large feet leaving clear prints in the snow.

"Was that a mountain lion?" Pete asked, his voice hushed.

Josh shook his head. "A lynx. It's really a treat to see one that close. They're very wary, secretive almost. And mostly nocturnal. Probably just finishing his night of hunting."

"And I suppose their hides are worth plenty." Josh turned at the sound of Shannon's voice.

"As a matter of fact, they are," he said dryly.

"So why don't you run after it and shoot it?"

Josh let out a sigh of exasperation. "Because, contrary to what you may think, I don't kill every living creature I see, just for the fun of it."

"Could have fooled me," was her curt reply.

Josh felt the anger move through him like a bitter wind. She was acting as judge and jury of him and his whole way of life. Not that it was a way of life he planned to hang on to indefinitely. But for now this was who he was.

He gave her a hard stare. Then he turned to Pete, making his face soften. "Let's have a look at those tracks."

"OK," he said willingly.

Josh forged through the snow, hearing only Pete's struggling footsteps behind him. Good, he thought. Let her stand there and freeze. Better yet, let her turn around and walk to the cabin. Maybe she'll get lost.

He stopped and knelt beside the lynx tracks, and Pete knelt beside him. Pointing his finger, he traced along the outline of a print.

"Look at the size of it. A lynx's feet act like snowshoes, distributing its weight so it can travel across deep snow. These fuzzy edges of the print are from the fur that covers each paw, right down to the ground."

"Have you ever caught one?"

Josh shook his head. "My dad has, but only two

the whole time we've been here. Like I said, they're elusive. But they're quite the prize. Their fur is soft as silk, and their meat is tender and tasty."

Pete looked thoughtful a moment. "Do you ever feel sorry—when you kill an animal, I mean?"

Josh looked Pete square in the eyes. "Sure I feel sorry. Anybody would. These animals are incredible. But we're not destroying them just for the sake of destroying them."

"Still, you like it, right? Hunting and trapping?"

"I like parts of it. There's the thrill of pursuing something, the suspense of waiting to see if you've succeeded. And there's the practical end of it, selling the furs, putting meat on the table."

Pete's face darkened. "Shannon doesn't eat meat," he said softly.

Josh took a deep breath. "I know. That's her choice. I wouldn't try to tell her how to live her life." He let the rest of his thought remain unspoken: So why should she tell me how to live mine?

They rose and turned back toward the creek. When they reached the machine, Shannon was already back in the sled, frosty as the cold December air.

10

*E*VER SINCE JOSH COULD REMEMBER, he'd thought of January as the longest month of the year. It was especially so at Willow Creek. For the few hours of daybreak, the sun hung distant and low, casting a hazy light stripped of warmth. Then each brief day stretched into an interminable night of unbroken darkness and quiet.

Temperatures dipped to thirty, then forty below, so even a brief trip to the outhouse made Josh's face sting with cold. Other than the squeak of dry snow beneath his boots, the woods resounded in utter silence, as every other creature stayed burrowed against the elements.

Josh stoked the woodstove each hour or so during the cold spell, fighting back the frigid air that seeped through the planks of the floor and into the cabin. A thick layer of frost crawled up the panes of the windows, and the cabin seemed to shrink, its walls bearing down upon them. They went to bed edgy and tense and woke feeling the same after countless hours of fitful sleep.

"I hope Nathan's doing all right in this cold," Josh's father worried. "We'd better go check on him."

"You can if you want," Josh snapped. "I'm not going out in this weather. He can take care of himself."

His father stared out the window at the drifted snow. "Just so he doesn't go and do something foolish, hiding out again where we can't find him."

"Now you're sounding just like him."

His dad turned, glaring. "What's that supposed to mean?"

Josh shrugged and looked away. He felt his lips twitch with the words. *Crazy. You're talking crazy, like Nathan.* He bit his lower lip, holding back the thoughts that clamored for voice.

"There's nothing wrong with Nathan," his dad challenged.

"I didn't say there was." Josh forced his words to sound calm and reasoned. "I only said you sounded just like him, making big deals out of nothing. Even Nathan wouldn't go off for no reason in this kind of weather."

His dad looked as if he were about to respond, then turned back toward the window.

"And wherever Nathan went before, it worked out fine," Josh reminded him. Nathan had returned happy from his time alone, his eyes bright with the excitement of whatever adventure he had enjoyed, though he would respond to none of his father's prodding about where he'd been.

Josh had the odd feeling that Shannon, of all people, knew about Nathan's hideout. The day after their trapping expedition, she had made a remark about following tracks on her own. But when Josh had pressed her for details about what kinds of tracks and where they had led, she refused to say any more about it. He would have chalked her silence up to her longing to protect an animal from his traps if it hadn't been for the comments she'd made about the lynx. On the day the Donaldsons were to leave, Pete had been retelling the encounter for Josh's father when Shannon added, "Nathan says some species of lynx are endangered."

Both Josh and his father had shot her a look. "You talked to Nathan again?" Josh asked.

Shannon flushed. "Right before he left," she explained. Strange, Josh thought, that they would have discussed the lynx before Shannon had even seen one.

But if Shannon knew of Nathan's whereabouts, she didn't say, and Josh didn't press her. He reminded himself that the mystery surrounding Nathan's hideaway was a weight that hung in the balance, ready to tip the scales of Josh's future. He needed to keep prodding at his father's worry, shaping it into a need to give the cabin to Nathan and move on to Wasilla.

That was one good thing about the cold spell, Josh realized. "Just so it's not this cold the next time the Donaldsons come." Josh spoke the words gently. "Then you would really have to worry about Nathan."

His dad turned abruptly from the window and pulled out a chair to sit at the table. "He'd have to swallow his pride and come stay with us if it were this cold," his father reasoned.

Josh shook his head. "I don't think we'll see Nathan swallow his pride, no matter how cold it gets. You've said it yourself, Dad. He's independent."

He watched the furrows form across his father's brow. "But it would be a life-and-death situation."

Josh shuddered inwardly, remembering the last life-and-death situation involving his brother—the bear. "I don't think Nathan finds death too high a price for his principles," Josh said quietly. "He loves the risk."

For a moment, Josh's father buried his face in his hands.

When he looked up, he admitted, "Maybe town is the best option for us, then. Let Nathan stay in this cabin by himself. Cut the risk." He shook his head. "I just don't know."

Josh forced himself to stifle the thrill of rising hope. He maintained his silence, letting his father's words sink back to their source. In his heart of hearts, Josh knew the only way his dream could come to pass would be if his father was sure it was best for his first-born. The younger son would have to be patient and wait.

He watched as his father wrapped himself in layers of jackets, coveralls, wool socks, boots, hats, scarves, mitten liners, and thick leather mittens. Frostbite could result from the slow quarter-mile walk to check on Nathan, but even if the machine would start, running it at these temperatures would be tough on the engine. His dad's mouth was set with grim determination. He would walk. He placed Nathan's well-being above his own comfort and safety.

Frigid air blasted into the cabin when his dad opened the door to leave. Josh felt the cold settle around him as the door shut, his father stepping wordless into the woods. He went to the window and watched the figure, small against the towering spruce, disappear down the trail.

The trees stood, stiff and motionless, in the dead calm of the arctic air. Days had passed since a squirrel last scurried from branch to branch or a chickadee last clung to a frosty twig. Each tree was a lonely sentinel against the cold, with sap thick and sluggish deep inside.

Josh laid a hand over the frosted glass, feeling the cold spread across his palm. He felt like one of those spruce, shut down by the cold, just barely alive. Hope, he reminded himself. There is hope, if Dad could only be convinced that our leaving would be good for Nathan.

But his hope faded like the fleeting winter daylight when his father returned.

"I don't know, Josh," he said, shaking his head. "He doesn't look good to me. Too thin."

"Nathan has always been thin."

"But now he has this gaunt, starved look about him. I asked him what he'd been eating lately. Said he couldn't remember, that it didn't matter."

Josh tried to think of how to turn this bit of information toward his purpose. "Maybe he's running short on supplies. If we left him here, with all of our food, and brought him provisions from town every so often, he'd do better." He drew in a deep breath and continued. "Did you suggest it to him—staying here, I mean, and us going to town?"

His dad shook his head. "It didn't seem right. Not with him like this."

Josh struggled for the logic of his reply. "But we're here now, and you say he's not doing well. So we're not helping much, are we? A change couldn't hurt."

"I just don't think he should be left alone. Not in

the dead of winter. Maybe come spring, or summer. But not now."

Josh felt the weight of the words settle in his chest. Spring or summer. Maybe. The dull routine, the emptiness, the loneliness of their existence, spread out before him like the endless wilderness. He had managed this long, resigned to the situation. But the faint light of hope had unsettled his darkness. He couldn't let it go.

He withdrew into silence, turning the matter over and over in his mind. He fell asleep considering the situation, examining the options, and awoke doing the same.

Three days passed. The cold spell broke, the thermometer climbing to ten below. And Josh had come to a conclusion: He would have to speak to Nathan himself. He would reason with him and get him to insist that they leave. Their father would listen to Nathan.

It was a simple plan, but it was made difficult by the fact that Josh had never cultivated any sort of relationship with Nathan. He had, in fact, avoided talking with Nathan any more than he had to. Nathan didn't care. He needed no one, least of all a little brother. Josh could only hope he'd listen and be convinced.

"OK if I take the machine and check my line?" Josh asked. He hoped his dad wouldn't want to come along.

His dad looked up from the dishes. "Go on ahead. I'll finish these and straighten up a bit. Maybe walk over to Nathan's."

Josh thought quickly. If his dad found him unexpectedly talking with Nathan, he might become suspicious. Better to avoid the surprise.

"I thought I'd stop by and see Nathan myself."

"Really?" His dad looked up from the soapy water, raising an eyebrow.

"See, I've got this report to do for my English class. On an American writer. I was thinking maybe I should do Thoreau. Nathan knows plenty about him."

A smile spread over his dad's face. "He sure does. I'm glad you're able to tap some of your brother's expertise. He'll be pleased."

Josh returned the smile. He was proud of himself for covering so well. He did have a report to do for English, but that was small compared to his real project, convincing Nathan.

It took a few pulls, but the snow machine started without any tinkering. Another good sign, Josh thought with satisfaction.

He wound his way through the trees under a crystal blue sky. The air, though brisk, felt invigorating after the long days inside. A faint breeze stirred the tops of the birches. Josh hoped it was a Chinook, the wind that brought warm air from the south once or twice each winter, a welcome reminder that the frigid cold wouldn't last forever.

He pulled the machine beside Harry's cabin and knocked loudly. The curtains were pulled tight and there was no sign of movement within. He pounded again and waited.

Finally, the door opened a crack. Josh could barely see Nathan's face through the darkness of the cabin.

"Josh?" Nathan's voice wavered.

"Could I come in?"

Nathan swung open the door. He stood, his long hair matted about his face, with a blanket wrapped around his slender frame.

Josh stepped inside and pulled off his boots. "Just woke up, did you?"

Nathan lifted a hand to rub his eyes. "Been sleeping a lot lately."

Josh took off his coat without waiting to be asked. He shivered in the chilly room. "Did your fire go out?"

Nathan yawned. "Guess so."

"Where's your wood pile? I'll help you stoke it."

Nathan pointed to two logs propped in a corner by the woodstove.

"That's it?" Josh asked. He reached for a log and opened the stove while Nathan looked on. Stirring the ashes, he set the log in the midst of a few glowing embers and watched until the fire took.

"Cold spell broke," he said, clamping the stove door shut. Nathan sat on the bed, barely visible in the darkened room, leaning against the wall, his knees tucked up to his chest. He looked like a child.

"Mind if I open the curtains?" Josh asked. Without waiting for a reply, he pulled aside one set. Morning light streamed in.

Nathan squinted. "Bright out there."

"Past time to rise and shine. You'd better get out there and cut some wood."

"Is that why you're here—to tell me what to do?"

This was the wrong way to start, with Nathan on the defensive. He'd have to change the subject, fast.

"Actually, I was hoping you might be able to help me out with a report I'm doing for correspondence. It's on Thoreau. I've got all the facts about his life, and I've read a chapter from *Walden*, but I'm stuck on his contributions to literature."

Nathan stroked his beard, the familiar gesture that showed he was thinking. The burning log in the stove crackled and popped. "His contributions. I've given that considerable thought. He made people stop and ponder nature and the wilderness."

Nathan paused. "But he sold them, and himself,

short." His words sounded angry. "After two years he gave in and went back to society. That's where he went wrong."

Josh felt the heavy weight of Nathan's stare, challenging him to respond. This wasn't going as he'd hoped.

"You won't find me making the same mistake," Nathan continued. "I've been figuring out ways to do it better."

"Better?"

"Living truly as part of nature. Without all of this."

Josh looked around to see what he could be referring to. "All of what?"

"All things manmade. Canned food and dried beans. Furniture. This cabin."

"But Nathan," Josh reasoned. "You have to eat."

Nathan shook his head. "Not out of cans. I'm eating as they do." He gestured toward the wall at the foot of his bed.

Josh saw that Nathan's collection of bear pictures and drawings had grown. There were several more photos, cut from magazines, of black bears in particular, along with more crude sketches of the animals. One sketch featured the full face of a bear with eyes that, though roughly drawn, seemed to stare right through Josh.

"They eat raw fish and berries," Josh said. "You can't get those in the winter."

"I've got some berries stored. That's what I'm eating now," Nathan said. The pride in his thin voice was unmistakable.

"Nathan, you're not an animal." Josh felt foolish stating the obvious. "You're not equipped like a bear for survival. You don't have the fur, the claws, the instincts."

"Little brother," Nathan said, a weak smile touching his lips. "Haven't you ever heard of those cases of children raised among wild animals? They take on the characteristics of the animals and thrive without any of the trappings of civilization."

"But you can't just go out and live with a bunch of bears."

Nathan's smile spread. *"Can't* is a word I've never had much use for."

Josh stifled the growing sense of alarm that rose inside him. He had to remember why he came. Through this tangle of crazy ideas, there had to be a way to convince Nathan to urge their father to leave. He took a deep breath.

"Dad's not going to let you do anything stupid, Nathan."

"He can't stop me."

"But he'll try. You know he will. He'll follow you through every phase of this plan of yours."

"There are places where he won't find me." The defiance was rising in Nathan's voice.

"Dad's a hunter. He tracks animals. You think he won't be able to find you and your animal friends?"

Josh paused, letting the words sink in. Nathan sat in silence, stroking his beard.

"Nate, there's only one way you're ever going to be able to do what you really want. Convince Dad you want our cabin. Get him to move back to town."

"But I don't want your cabin. I don't want any cabin. I want to live out there." Nathan nodded toward the window.

Josh struggled with the rising river of guilt that stormed his insides. Nathan wouldn't last the winter if he carried on this way. To try was utter foolishness. Suicidal. Their dad was right. Nathan needed them to look after him until he came to his senses.

If he came to his senses, Josh reasoned. He could go off in the woods and never return, even with them close by. He'd made his determination clear. Didn't he have a right to do as he chose, even if it was crazy? And if they couldn't stop him, why should they hang on here?

"Just say you want the cabin, Nate. You don't have to actually live there. Just get us out of the way."

The thin smile returned to Nathan's face. "You'd like that, wouldn't you? You've never really taken to the wilderness."

Josh struggled against the smug sound of his brother's voice. He wouldn't defend himself, pointing out how much he had adjusted, all things considered, how it was more than crazy to want to live among animals instead of people. None of that would serve his purpose.

"I guess not, Nathan. Not like you have. I'm sure you'll do fine on your own." He swallowed hard. "But you'll never really know while Dad and I are here. Dad won't let you find out."

Josh stood and zipped his coat. He'd said enough, too much perhaps.

Nathan stayed where he sat, stroking his beard. "Maybe you're right, little brother. Maybe you're right."

11

$\mathcal{A}$ LONG SILENCE on the subject set in. Josh knew his dad was still worried about his older son; he checked on him daily now. And Josh knew he had reason to worry. Even as he waited to hear whether Nathan would suggest that they leave, he struggled with his guilt over planting the idea. But he reminded himself that Nathan would do whatever he wanted. He always did.

The following week when they went to Wasilla to sell furs, Josh and his father sat at a table in the same fast-food restaurant they'd visited months earlier. Josh recalled the group of high school students he'd watched with envy. Today their table, and most of the restaurant, was empty. A gray-haired woman hummed softly as she wiped the remains of the noon rush from the countertop. Fluorescent lights buzzed overhead.

Josh's father pushed aside his tray and spread a copy of the thin Wasilla weekly in front of him. Josh sipped a thick chocolate shake through his straw. He forced himself to focus on the sweet, syrupy flavor, not the hope that surged inside. His father had the paper open to the classifieds.

"Damn apartments start at six-fifty a month," his father grumbled.

"What about jobs?" Josh prompted.

"Let's see. Here's one: 'Handyman needed for light maintenance and repairs. References required. Townhouse Square.'"

"Townhouse Square. Sounds like an apartment complex. Maybe we'd get a break on the rent."

"Maybe." Josh's father sighed and closed the paper. "Don't know what I'd do about references, though. Been away from working for a while."

Josh noisily sipped the last of the shake from the paper cup. "There's the guy you worked for down in Anchorage."

"If he's still around."

"And what about Frank Donaldson? I'll bet he'd let you use him as a reference."

His father pushed the paper aside. "That's another thing. They should be back next week. Got to see if Frank would look in on Nathan when he's out there with his family."

His plan sounded definite. Nathan must have spoken to their dad about the cabin.

"So you decided it would be better for Nathan after all to have our place?" Josh hoped his voice sounded casual, as if he were asking about the weather.

Josh's father swallowed the last of his coffee. "Actually, Nathan decided. Says he'd feel more comfortable at our cabin."

He got up to leave. "Nate needs some kind of change, that's for sure." His voice was grim.

"Aren't you taking that with you?" Josh asked, nodding toward the paper. "Maybe you should call about that handyman job before we leave town."

His father tucked the paper under his arm. "No need to make any calls yet. One thing at a time."

Josh knew better than to dwell on the subject of leaving. It could end up being one more deflated dream, when it came down to actually happening. And if he seemed too eager, his dad might suspect his involvement in Nathan's sudden interest in their cabin. The less said, the better.

But when his father suggested they talk with Frank on the first day the Donaldsons were due back, Josh allowed himself a small helping of hope. He pushed aside his lingering guilt over leaving Nathan alone in the wilderness. Nathan would do whatever Nathan chose, he told himself again, be it with or without them.

After exchanging the usual pleasantries, his dad broached the subject.

"Say, Frank." Josh's father looked down, then back up at Frank. "Josh and I are thinking of moving to town. Wasilla. We'd let Nathan have our place. 'Course, we'd like to come on some weekends, see how he's doing. Think Harry would let us stay here once in a while?"

Frank shrugged. "Don't know why not. Got to missing the city life, did you?"

Shannon looked up at the mention of city life.

"Yes and no. Josh does, for sure."

Her brown eyes caught Josh's, and she gave him a quizzical look.

"Oh, boy," Pete exclaimed. "You're moving to Anchorage, Josh? You could be our neighbors."

"Not Anchorage. Wasilla. We're thinking of moving to Wasilla." Josh felt lighter just speaking the words.

"Hey, Josh. Dad and I brought our skates. Will you go skating with me?" Pete asked.

"Hope you brought your shovel, too. We'll have to clear a spot."

"There's one on the porch, and I like to shovel."

Josh grinned. "Good enough. I'll come back with my skates and our shovel. But even with the two of us, it will take a lot of shoveling."

"I'll help." Josh stared at Shannon as she continued. "Dad's got another shovel in the back of his truck. It would be something to do."

"Suit yourself," Josh said with a shrug. It couldn't

be any worse than having her tag along on the trapline.

Josh returned by snow machine, racing along the trail, exuberant. His dad must be serious after all, to bring the plan up with Frank. He wondered how long it would take to pack up and leave. They didn't have much.

He sat Shannon on the back of the machine this time and put Pete in the sled, along with the shovel and two hockey sticks, which had been gathering dust in a corner of their porch. He'd almost forgotten he had them. With the discovery of the sticks, he'd climbed back to the loft and dug the puck from the bottom of his wooden crate.

After an hour of hard shoveling, Josh, Pete, and Shannon had a ten-by-twenty patch of ice cleared on the pond, with snow banked up around the edges of the tiny rink. The three of them, still breathing heavily and their cheeks rosy with the effort, sat on a snow pile and took off their boots.

Pete's new skates fit fine, but Josh and Shannon ended up trading the too-big skates she had borrowed from Frank for Josh's too-small skates he'd dug out of a box on the porch.

"You skated much before?" Josh asked Pete as he pulled the laces tight for him.

"Not much. And I never played hockey. Dad took me to some semipro games, though. It's cool."

Josh smiled. "It is. If I'm not too rusty, I'll show you a few moves. These tight enough?"

Pete nodded.

"How about yours?" he asked Shannon.

"Good enough, I guess. I've never put on a pair of skates before."

Josh yielded to a little smile. He had to give her credit there. Most girls he'd known wouldn't embarrass themselves trying to skate for the first time in front of someone else. But then she wouldn't be trying to impress him.

Josh's first few strides across the tiny rink felt foreign, but he quickly regained his fast, even pace. The surface was surprisingly smooth, thanks to a solid freeze back in November before the snow fell. On his second lap around, Josh stopped abruptly in front of Pete, spraying a rooster tail of ice particles into the air.

Pete stood, wobbling slightly on his new skates. "Wow, you're fast," he said.

Josh grinned and reached out a hand. "Come on. I'll show you a few tricks."

He gave Pete a quick lesson in power skating, showing him how to use the upper muscles of his legs rather than his feet to propel him forward. "Now you try a few laps on your own," he said, giving the boy a small push. Then he skated over to Shannon, who was making a few hesitant glides along the rink's edge.

"You'll get cold if you don't move any faster than that," he chided. He reached out a hand.

She held on tight, and he pulled her along for the length of the rink. She teetered beside him, her balance uncertain. When they reached the end of the ice, he tried letting go, but she ended up on her backside.

"Let's try it again," Josh said, holding out both hands for her to grasp. "You've got to find your own center of gravity and hold on to it. And use your edges. Those skates are a little dull, but you still should be able to catch an edge. That's the only way you'll be able to maneuver and turn."

"Turn?" Her eyes looked bigger than usual.

"Sure. It's not that tough. You've just got to get comfortable with shifting your weight from one skate to the other."

"One skate? I'm not doing so well with two." She smiled as she said it. The hair around her face as well as her eyelashes was growing frosty.

"Here, I'll hold you steady," Josh said, circling his arm around her waist. "Right foot first. Glide! Now left. Glide!"

He was almost sorry when she caught on quickly and he was able to let go of her after only a few laps. The wobble was gone, and she skated confidently, though slowly, around the rink.

Josh grabbed one of the sticks and pulled out the

puck he had stuffed in his pocket. He sped up and down the tiny rink, swiping at the puck with a steady rhythm of his stick, taking the corners, switching to a backward stride without ever losing control of the black disk. He was surprised at how quickly it all came back to him, not just his stride and stick handling but the thrill of motion and precise control.

He stopped hard at the end of the rink, breathing heavily. It was like the hard stop at center ice, with the crowd cheering at his name called out in the starting lineup. "And at center, Josh Harris." He could almost hear the announcer's booming voice. What would it be like playing now, not just in a recreational league, but for a high school team, with his classmates cheering in the stands?

He used the blade of his stick to draw goal pipes in the pile of snow at the end of the rink. Then he backed up and practiced shooting. Hard on the ice right corner, hard on the ice left corner, wrist shot, slap shot, high to the left, high to the right. They were all still there, the shots he had worked so hard to master, the shots that had made him one of his team's leading scorers. Before long he'd have a chance to prove himself again on a real rink.

Pete skated alongside him, holding the other stick out in front of him. "Can you teach me to play?"

Josh grinned. "Not in one afternoon. But here, I'll show you some shots."

He showed Pete how to hold the stick and turn the blade to control the puck. He had him practice shot after shot into the make-believe net.

"Not bad," he said finally. "Not bad at all. Make sure your dad gets you a stick the right size when you go home, and keep practicing. I'll be coming down to watch you play for one of those semipro teams someday."

Shannon grabbed at his hand. "One more time around the rink with me, and then we'd better go. I'm starting to lose feeling in my toes."

Josh skated beside her, slowing his pace to match her steady stride. For that moment, it was hard to believe that harsh words had ever passed between them.

When they got back to Harry's cabin, Josh's father was sitting at the table with Frank.

"Made a pot of chili and invited your dad over to share it," Frank explained. The warm, spicy smell filled the cabin.

"I'm starved," Pete exclaimed, dropping his snow-suit to the floor.

"Not starved," Shannon corrected. She picked up the snowsuit and shook the drips from it. "Just hungry."

"Whichever," Josh said. "I am, too."

They sat around the table, and Josh let the satisfying warmth of the chili fill his stomach. Pete and

Shannon laughed with their dad, exaggerating all the effort of clearing the rink and learning to skate. Even Josh's father was smiling as he took in their conversation.

This must be what it's like to have a real family, Josh thought. He looked over at Shannon. Her dark hair gleamed in the light of the lantern, and her face still glowed from being outdoors. He wondered if she took after her mother, in looks and in her serious way of taking care of things, whether it was Pete's snowsuit or the balance of the ecosystem.

After dinner was through and the dishes washed, dried, and put away, Shannon slipped out to the outhouse and Josh and his father prepared to leave. Josh was happy to hear his father going over the Wasilla plan once more with Frank.

"And if on the weekends when you're here, you can look in on Nathan, we'd be much obliged."

Nathan. They'd gone all night without mentioning his name, and everything had seemed so right. Josh knew he should feel bad, thinking that way about his brother, but he was tired of feeling bad about Nathan. Instead, growing warm in his zipped parka, he stepped outside to wait for his father.

He stood on the cabin steps and looked up into the blackened sky. It was a rare night of warmer air—around zero, most likely—with no clouds yet obscuring the stars. Hands in the pockets of his parka, he searched until he located the North Star, the one point around which all the constellations seemed to revolve. As he stood staring, a flickering band of green light began to work its way across the sky.

Josh heard the crunch of footsteps and looked down. Shannon was picking her way through the snow, back toward the spot where he stood.

She slowed when she reached him. Her brown eyes looked even softer in the starlight. "Look!" He pointed with one hand toward the sky. High overhead, the flicker of green had grown to a stream of shimmering green, pink, and purple that danced among the stars.

Shannon gasped. "I've never seen anything like it." Her voice was barely a whisper.

Josh felt an odd thrill move through him. The eerie spectacle of the aurora always seemed like a living thing.

"The colors are incredible," Shannon said.

Josh nodded. "You're lucky. This is one of the best displays I've ever seen."

"They aren't like this in Anchorage," Shannon whispered.

"Too many lights," Josh said.

For a fleeting moment, Josh felt her eyes on him. "Why would you want to go back to the city and miss this?" she asked. "And not just this. Everything—the fresh air, the pure white snow, the total quiet."

Josh looked down and caught her eye. There was no explaining what she, a sometime visitor to the wilderness, would never fully understand: the bitter cold of winter, the swarming bugs of summer, the way nature rose up and challenged you at every turn, the aching feeling of being alone day after day with no one to share your deepest thoughts and longings.

"It'll be better for Nathan if we leave," he said. He turned his eyes back to the sky. The lights were fading as quickly as they'd grown, shrinking to a single wave of flickering green.

"Nathan's fine," Shannon said quietly. "He doesn't need your cabin."

Josh turned his face back toward hers. "You don't see him all the time. He needs a change. And my dad—he worries about Nathan. Like now. When he's out there somewhere."

"He's fine," she repeated. "I can't tell you any more than that. But really, he's fine."

Josh stared at her. It was as he suspected. She knew where Nathan hid. Not that it mattered, but he wanted to know more.

Just then the cabin door opened, and his father came out. "Sorry to keep you waiting," he said.

Josh gave Shannon a final look. Her lips were pressed together in a tight, unwavering line. Even if they'd had all the time in the world, she wouldn't have given up Nathan's secret.

12

$\mathcal{A}$s the days grew longer and light streamed through the cabin windows for seven hours at a time, Josh allowed his hope to surge, like a tiny plant struggling out of its seed. His father had laid out their plan to Frank, and all that remained was word that Harry would let them use his cabin occasionally, to check on Nathan.

"Nate, you'll have your own place before long," their father told him soon after the Donaldsons left.

"My place," Nathan said. His words were hardly a reply.

Josh glanced at Nathan's bear wall. The collage of pictures had grown, with more carefully printed quotes sprinkled among the photos and drawings. *Live the dream to its fullest,* read one. *Look in its eyes and see yourself,* said another. The new quotes were not attributed. Josh wondered if they were Nathan's own words.

Josh felt Nathan's eyes on him as he studied the wall. "Impressive creatures, aren't they?" Nathan asked.

"Powerful," Josh said. The smell of the charging

bear and the hot look in its eyes as it tumbled toward him that October day remained vivid in his memory.

"Someday you'll understand, little brother," Nathan said.

Checking on Nathan remained a daily occurrence. Josh hoped that didn't mean that his dad was rethinking the decision to leave. Often when they stopped by Harry's cabin, Nathan was gone.

"Where do you suppose he goes?" their father wondered aloud one day.

Josh shrugged. "At least he's out. Like you always say, fresh air's good for a person."

"True," his father conceded. "But I can't figure what purpose he'd have, out there wandering around."

"Getting water or wood maybe, or just enjoying nature. He likes that," Josh said.

Even Josh had to admit Willow Creek grew more beautiful as February slid into March. The sun brought some warmth to the air, and it reflected off the snow with an almost blinding brightness. Gone were the pale shades of midwinter, replaced by a sky of penetrating blue that framed the towering Alaska Range in the distance.

Josh had begun tracking the calendar, making invisible X's in his mind, counting down the days until the Donaldsons would return with the word that would make their plans final. Twenty-eight shrank quickly to twenty and then to ten.

He attacked his correspondence lessons with new vigor, sometimes working late into the night by lantern light. He wanted to be up with the rest of the class when he entered high school.

High school. What would it be like? The last time he'd been in school, in seventh grade, high school seemed a foreign world. Soon, if all went well, it would be the stuff of his everyday existence. Even algebra wasn't going to keep him from enjoying it.

He pictured himself in a red-and-white school jacket, like the ones the boys had been wearing in the restaurant that day long ago. In a year or two, maybe he'd have a tiny gold hockey player pinned to a letter. And maybe a girl would look up at him with admiration, as he'd seen the girls look at the boys in the restaurant.

When the countdown finally reached two, Josh spent a long day outside, pulling his traps and snares. The season was nearly over anyhow. Animals would be mating soon, and the furs would turn scraggly and rough. As he sprung each trap and lifted it from its carefully concealed spot, he brushed snow and branches back to cover the area where the trap had sat. Over and over, he erased the tiny marks he'd made in the vast wilderness.

His pack grew heavier with the weight of the metal, and eventually he had to leave it in the sled. He pulled in two mink, a marten, and a fox as well.

That evening he brought the lantern onto the porch and sliced down the belly of each of the stiff animals, peeling the skin carefully back from each one. Stripped of their fur, the carcasses were gruesome red things, lifeless eyes staring out from glistening flesh.

Josh looked away from the spot where he'd left the carcasses spread on a sheet of newspaper and turned his attention to pulling each skin over a stretcher. He remembered what he'd learned somewhere, that Native Americans used to thank the animals for giving themselves up to humans. The whispered words formed in his mind. *Thank you, mink. Thank you, marten. Thank you, fox.*

He pulled the last skin carefully over the stretcher and shook his head. Talking to dead animals wasn't the kind of behavior that would make him a popular guy at Wasilla High. Still, he was grateful for the furs. The money they'd get from selling them would buy a week's worth of groceries, to get him and his father started with their new life.

Josh brought the stretchers in one at a time, propping each beside the other along the wall near the door. He brought the lantern in last of all. Added to the glow of the second lantern, next to where his father sat paging through a magazine, its light made the cabin nearly as bright as a city house would be.

His father looked up from the magazine and studied the fruits of Josh's labor. "Some nice pelts there," he said.

Josh smiled. "With the ones you brought in yesterday, we should have enough money to get started in Wasilla."

"I suppose we will," his father said, but worry clouded his eyes. He rubbed at his forehead a moment. Josh sank into the overstuffed chair beside the sofa.

"Dad, it's going to work out. Nathan will be fine."

His father looked up at him. "I guess he will be. He needs his space. And there's nothing much I can do for him here. Just check up on him once in a while. I just don't ever want to lose touch with him again."

"I know, Dad," Josh said quietly.

"But what about us?"

The question took Josh by surprise. "Us?"

"It won't be the same in town. I'll be working. You'll be in school. We'll each have our own lives."

How could he tell his father that his own life was precisely what he'd been longing for? His own life, filled with school and cars and friends. His own life, with movies to see and games to play. His own life.

Josh shifted where he sat. "We'll be coming back

to Willow Creek on weekends. Some weekends, any-how."

His father shook his head. "Not the same. The world, as the great poet said, will be too much with us."

It was the first time Josh had heard his father quote poetry. He wasn't quite sure what he meant. Silence settled around them, except for the crackling of the wood in the stove. A heavy weariness came over Josh. Another day had come to an end. He looked at the calendar and made an invisible *X* in his mind.

Josh awoke the next morning with the same thought he had savored when he'd fallen asleep. One more day. He started to push the sheet and blankets from his body, then pulled them up again as he felt the chill of the air. His father must have forgotten to stoke the fire.

Tomorrow he would wake and bundle the bed coverings to take to Wasilla. He looked around the loft. There would be little else to pack. The clothes in the corner all needed washing. A Laundromat would have to be one of their first stops.

He rolled up on one elbow and looked into the wooden crate filled with the few possessions that had traveled with them as he and his father had moved from state to state. He reached inside, sifting through the items with one hand. Funny how when you didn't own much, each possession seemed more valuable.

Nathan had proclaimed it would be just the opposite—living in the wilderness would make material possessions seem meaningless. Only the struggle for survival would matter. Perhaps it had worked that way for Nathan, but not for Josh.

His fingers passed over the wood-framed photo, the hockey programs, the puck. They came to rest on a spiral notebook, its paper cover tattered and worn. With a yank, Josh pulled it to the top of the crate. He lay back and held the open notebook overhead, flipping through pages of words and pictures.

It was like turning pages of his past. His father had bought the notebook years ago at a convenience store, to give his restless son something to do as they drove farther and farther west. Josh saw his own childish renderings of cars and trucks they had passed along the way. He'd drawn mountains when they reached the Rockies and ocean waves when they reached Puget Sound.

The drawings, though still not artful, looked at least less childish by the middle of the notebook, when their journeys took them north to Alaska on the Al–Can Highway. His subjects became more animate: a beaver that had waddled across the gravel road, a grouse that had flown up and nearly hit their windshield.

There were words on the last few pages of the notebook. He'd written them when they'd first come to Willow Creek, out of boredom, with the idea of keeping a journal. There was even one attempt at a poem. But his entries were for the most part all too plain and typical. "Hauled water. Washed clothes. Lots of work. Bugs are horrible. Bites everywhere."

Josh shut the notebook and slid it back inside the crate. He sat up and felt the goose bumps spread across his chest. It was cold.

He pulled on a full set of long johns and a pair of wool socks before donning his jeans and flannel shirt. He'd be needing money for clothes. Most likely they weren't wearing flannel at Wasilla High. He'd check it out, see what was in style, then get an after-school job somewhere. His father would have enough to worry about, just putting food on the table.

Josh climbed down the ladder. It was even colder downstairs, except for a ring of warmth around the stove. He stood next to his father there.

"Forget to stoke it, Dad?"

His father shook his head. "Look at the thermometer. Bitter cold out."

Josh went to the window, where frost was already beginning to form on the lower panes. "Thirty below." His heart sank as he said the words. Starting the truck would be a problem unless the cold spell proved short-lived.

He rubbed his hands together.

"Put extra wood on when I got up," his father said. "Should get back up to tolerable in here before long."

Josh was still pondering the truck. If they had electricity, they could plug in the oil pan heater as they used to do in Anchorage. If they had electricity.

"Got to go after Nathan. Unless he's got a real warm place, he'd better stay the night here, not head for wherever he goes when the Donaldsons come. Not fit for man or beast out."

Josh barely acknowledged his father. He'd heard of people starting a little fire under a vehicle to warm it up. And the Donaldsons—surely they'd have jumper cables.

It was late in the day by the time they got things put away at their cabin. They packed dishes, pots, and pans in one box, leaving a few for Nathan. In another box, they stacked some canned goods, but his father wanted to leave most of the food for his older son. Josh was careful not to mention that Nathan probably wouldn't eat it. The last thing Josh needed now was for his dad to start worrying and change his mind.

His father stuffed a few favorite books in the bottom of his duffel bag. "Read those magazines three times each, at least," he said, nodding toward the stack they left near the sofa.

"Good thing we took care of the traps while it was

warmer. Thirty below in March." His father shook his head.

The time came to go after Nathan. They decided to try to start the snow machine. It had to be coaxed with starting fluid and a lot of priming, but eventually it came to life. They hitched the sled behind and braced against the cold as they sped toward Harry's place.

"I'm leaving it running," Josh's father said over the idle of the engine. "Only take a minute to get Nathan."

Josh waited, straddling the seat, thumb on the throttle to rev the engine when it started to fade. His fingertips began to sting. *Hurry up,* he urged silently.

But when his father returned, it was without Nathan. Josh got up and stood close, so he could hear his father's explanation.

His father's words were brief and grim. "He's gone."

13

"Gone? But where would he go in this cold?" Josh hit the kill switch as he spoke and found himself yelling the words.

His father took a deep breath. "It's like him to take a risk, to see if he could survive in these extreme conditions."

Josh stomped his feet to bring warmth to his toes. "Maybe he just went out for a while, to get water or something."

"Could be." His father's eyes spanned the woods. "Mighty cold for an errand."

"We can go looking," Josh suggested, ignoring the sting of cold on his face. "While it's still light out."

His father looked at the ground. "Tracks everywhere. No telling which way he went."

Josh studied the ground. It hadn't snowed in weeks, and Nathan had made many trips down to the creek and into the woods, from the looks of the tracks. There was no way of knowing which had been made most recently.

"We won't find him standing here." Josh pulled

the rope to start the engine. "I'll drive, and you look," he suggested.

His father climbed on behind him and they took off. Josh drove slowly, giving his father time to scan the edges of the trail, turning whenever his father tapped him on the shoulder and pointed.

The churning mix of irritation and disappointment Josh felt inside left little room for the concern he knew he should feel for his brother. How could Nathan do this, when they were just on the verge of being free of this place? Why did his stupid moves always have to wreak havoc in their lives? If he had to take yet another risk to prove something to himself, couldn't he have waited a day or two, until after they were gone?

When they reached the meadow, his father yelled at him to stop. Josh shut down the machine and stood beside his father. They stared across the flat stretch of snow toward the mountains, tinged pink with the fading sunset. In the dim light, it was hard to tell where tracks, old or new, cut through the open space.

The stinging in Josh's fingers turned to a dull ache. He shook his wrists, forcing the blood to move faster.

"He's probably safe and warm in some old shack only he knows about, back in toward the mountains," Josh said. "A place where he's gone those other times the Donaldsons came."

His father scanned the horizon. "No smoke. Have to have a fire going in this cold."

"Maybe it just went out. He can start another. People camp in winter, after all. He'll come in if he gets too cold."

His father shook his head. "Doesn't make sense. Told him we'd be leaving, long as Harry gave his OK. Why go out now?"

Josh had long ago given up trying to make sense of Nathan. "Maybe he didn't understand that we meant to leave right away. Or maybe he just wanted to do whatever he does, wherever he goes, one more time. Before he starts over at our place."

His father shifted, stomping at the frozen ground.

"Maybe he's back by now," Josh suggested.

He watched his father scan the perimeter of the darkening meadow. "Maybe he is. Let's go." His father's voice was small and distant.

But the darkened windows of Harry's cabin gave them little cause for hope. When they pushed open the door, they found the air had grown frosty.

"Let's get a fire going," Josh suggested. "If—when—he comes back, he'll be cold."

He piled logs over the cold ashes, and his father lit a blaze. They stood beside the stove, warming their hands and toes.

"You don't suppose he could be at our place?

Maybe our paths crossed," Josh's father suggested.

"Could be," Josh said.

After stoking the fire with more logs, they headed back to their cabin. But even before they reached it, Josh could see that no lanterns were lit, and only a wisp of smoke trailed from the chimney.

The quiet pressed in around them. They picked at bits of leftover stew and biscuits, warmed on the stove. After supper, Josh's father paced in front of the window, stopping every so often to stare at the thermometer, which still hung without wavering at the thirty-below mark.

Josh put a hand on his father's shoulder. His father, who usually held his shoulders solid and square, now let them slump as if in defeat.

"Dad, Nathan is tough. He's a survivor."

His father nodded. "All those years without a father. I guess they made him tough."

Josh turned away. There was something in his father's pain that stabbed deep within, something he couldn't put a name on. The only thought that came was an unspoken question. Would his father ever care this much about him?

"If only we had some idea of where to look." There was a quiver in his father's voice.

Josh swallowed hard. Perhaps he should have said it earlier. "Shannon."

"Shannon?"

"I think she knows where Nathan stays."

"But how could she?"

"I don't know for sure. But she sort of let on that she followed him one time. Sounded like she maybe talked to him even." Josh felt the last of his energy drain with the words. It was as much as admitting that he hadn't much tried to track Nathan, back in the beginning when his father had wanted him to search.

But if his father felt betrayed, his face didn't show it. Instead, he grasped at the thin line of hope Josh had thrown him. "Shannon. Well, then, we'll be able to ask her tomorrow. We'll go over first thing in the morning and wait for them."

"And Nathan could be back by morning." It was completely possible. Nathan would tire of tangling with the arctic air and retreat to the cabin. As long as he didn't know they'd been looking for him, his pride would be intact.

But in the morning Nathan was still gone. They headed for Harry's cabin first thing and found it as empty as it had been the night before. Josh stoked the fire and put on a pot of coffee. Then they waited.

The waiting seemed interminable. Josh felt the weariness of a night of fitful sleep, and worse, of his hopes hanging in the balance. Judging by his father's haggard look, he hadn't slept at all.

The only bright spot was the mercury, which crept up to twenty below. It was hardly a heat wave, but the extra ten degrees might make a difference in Nathan's struggle for survival. And it would make looking for him more tolerable, especially if Shannon could help them focus their search.

Josh hoped she really did know something. He knew he could be putting too much stock in her vague reassurances about his brother.

At the rumble of the truck, Josh and his father jumped to their feet. They waited on the steps, cold seeping through their flannel shirts, as the Donaldsons climbed out.

"Good morning to you," Frank said cheerfully. The worried looks on their faces must have betrayed them, for he quickly added, "I hope everything's all right."

"Actually, we're concerned about Nathan. It's been real cold, and he's nowhere to be found."

Frank helped Pete down from the truck, and Shannon crawled out behind him.

"We thought your girl might be able to give us some idea of where to find him," Josh's father continued.

Shannon shot a look at Josh.

"Shannon?" Frank said. He looked back at his daughter. "You know something about where Nathan stays?"

She looked down a moment and then up again, her lips set firmly, her eyes resolute. "Is he in any danger?"

Josh's father opened the door for them. "We think he may be. He's been out for about twenty-four hours now."

"At least," Josh added. He looked Shannon square in the eye.

"But he's been out longer than that before."

"Thirty below, yesterday and last night," Josh's father said grimly.

"Too cold, unless you know he's somewhere plenty warm," Josh prodded.

They stood inside the cabin door. Shannon's eyes wavered from Josh to his father and back again. "He—he says he stays warm enough."

"But both other times it's been above zero. This is thirty below. We're talking frostbite, hypothermia." Josh made no attempt to cover the irritation in his voice. "Hypothermia distorts judgment. Freezing victims sometimes peel off their clothes or start to wander aimlessly."

"Josh is right," his father added. "It's important that if you know something about where Nathan might be, you tell us."

Shannon pulled off her hat and played with the tassel. "He asked me not to tell anyone where he stayed."

Josh looked her in the eye. "All right, then," he said slowly. "If you can't tell us, just show us. We can stay back. You can go in and make sure he's OK. He wouldn't mind that, would he?"

"I guess not." She hesitated. "I hope I can find it again. It's been a while."

She pulled her hat back on and followed Josh and his father through the door. Josh started for the snow machine.

"I don't think that would be such a good idea," she said. Josh looked at her. "The machine, I mean. I'd better walk, like I did before. So I can find the way. It's not that far."

"OK, Shannon," Josh's father said. "Just so you can find it. We'll follow behind."

They set off at a brisk pace, following a moose trail through the trees. The trail narrowed to a series of footprints in the deep snow, and as they wound their way through the willow shrubs, it became clear that the machine couldn't have maneuvered very well along the path she had chosen. Josh hoped she knew where she was going.

They'd been on the trail for half an hour when Shannon paused and looked around her. "I can't quite remember whether the turn is here or up ahead a ways."

She really had no sense of the danger in these woods, Josh realized. She could get lost and wander for days. While she pondered the trail, he looked around for his own landmarks. Behind them, a tall spruce stood out from the others, marking a spot between them and the cabin. Along the ground to their right, snow covered a fallen birch. And with the morning sun at their backs, they were headed almost due west. She wasn't going to get him lost.

She shook her head. "It's either straight ahead and then to the right, or to the right and then straight ahead."

"How about if you lead Josh straight ahead and I'll try to the right?" his father suggested. "That is, if you can tell me what we're looking for and about how far."

"I think it's only about fifteen minutes from here. You go down, in this sort of steep ditch."

The ravine, Josh thought. It was where Josh had seen the tracks but hadn't followed. It was steep, all right, but from this part of the woods it was hard to tell in which direction it lay. They could have gotten close on the machine, he thought with a twist of irritation, if she had only given them some information.

"And we're looking for?" Josh's father prodded.

"It's a den. An old bear den. Dug out in the side of the ditch. It's covered with a lot of branches. You'll have to look close."

An old bear den. It made sense, Josh thought. Dug into the earth and covered with snow and branches, it would be halfway warm. But he couldn't have a fire in there. Josh doubted it would be warm enough at thirty below, except for a bear.

"But you won't disturb him?" Shannon reminded his father. "You won't give yourself away?"

"I won't. Let's meet back at this spot in a half hour or so. If the den's down my trail, I'll take you back in after him."

Shannon nodded, then looked around at the spot where they stood.

"I'll remember this place," Josh said. "You go on ahead."

After five minutes of steady walking, they began a gradual descent. Ten minutes later, they were standing at the bottom of the ravine.

Josh stood beside Shannon. He could hear her working to steady her breath after the exertion of the trail, and he waited a moment before asking, "Is this it?"

His voice rang from the sides of the ravine. Shannon lifted a finger to her lips. "Shhh!" she warned. She stepped back into the brush and pointed. "Right there," she whispered.

Josh looked beyond her pointing finger to a snowy pile of brush along the side of the ravine. "In there?" he asked. She nodded, motioning for him to join her in the trees.

It was annoying, the way she acted like Nathan was an animal they had to be careful not to flush out of hiding. But he crouched down among the willows while she picked her way toward the bank.

"Nathan?" he heard her say softly. She pulled aside a few branches and peered into the cavern.

She stood straight and looked back at Josh. "Not there." She mouthed the words.

Josh crawled from his hiding place. "Now what?" he asked.

She waved him forward. "There's one other spot," she said, her voice still low. "Around that bend."

Josh followed as she picked her way along the bottom of the ravine. At the bend, she knelt and pointed. "Over there."

He peered around the bend but saw nothing except a jumble of rocks and branches. "You think he's over there someplace?"

"He brought me here once," Shannon whispered.

Josh couldn't imagine why. There was nothing to see. He shifted his weight from one crouched leg to another. The cold seeped through his jeans and long johns to his skin. Coveralls would have been a better choice for what was turning into an all-day expedition. Not that they had all day. They needed to get back to the meeting point with his father.

He stood suddenly and yelled. "Nathan!" His voice

echoed through the ravine. He felt a satisfaction in its loud, angry tone, even if Nathan couldn't hear him. "Nathan! Quit playing like an animal!"

"Josh!" Shannon stood beside him, her eyes filled with horror.

In the same instant, he heard a pained, angry growl.

14

SNOW AND BRANCHES went flying from the spot where Shannon had pointed, exposing a dark, cavernous opening. Then the darkness shook, and Josh realized that it was a bear.

He stepped back around the bend, his heart beating wildly, the memory of the October bear as fresh as if it had been last week. He heard Shannon gasp.

He put a hand on her arm. "Stay still," he said, his voice a rough whisper. "I don't think it can see us."

Then he crouched and peered through the branches of a willow that grew nearly straight out from the bank.

The bear shook its head slowly from side to side, as if trying to bring life back into focus from its deep winter sleep. Not ten yards away from the drowsy bear, crouched on all fours, was Nathan.

It was like a bad dream, where the worst pieces come together at the worst moments. Where had Nathan been hiding? The question was no more than a fleeting thought. Josh watched, horrified, as the bear fixed its eyes on his brother.

Shock shone in Nathan's eyes as he stared up at the fierce creature. Still crouching, he eased slowly backward. The bear followed Nathan's careful movements. For a split second, it looked back at the cavern. Two sets of gleaming eyes peered out of the darkness, almost at ground level. Cubs, Josh realized. She's defending her cubs.

The she-bear turned back toward Nathan, her lips drawn over her teeth in a snarl. Nathan continued creeping backward. Another five yards came between him and the sow.

Then, in an instant, the bear lunged at Nathan. Nathan covered his head with his arms. Josh froze in terror as the bear bit first at one arm, then at another. Blood flowed instantly from the wounds.

Josh tried to think. He had no gun. He could make noise, distract the bear. But her instinct to protect her cubs would send her charging in his direction. Shannon's direction. And then what?

The sow reared up on her hind legs, her claws fully exposed. She turned back to look at the tiny eyes watching her from the den. Then she lunged again at Nathan, biting into his right shoulder and lifting his body three feet from the ground. She shook him, like a cat playing with a mouse before going for the final kill.

At the sound of a faint mewing from the den, the bear opened her jaws, and Nathan fell to the ground.

She studied him where he lay, motionless. Then she dropped to all fours and ran to the den. She crawled inside, and the tiny cub eyes disappeared.

Nathan lay like a discarded toy, except for the blood that flowed from wounds in both arms and his right shoulder to stain the snow beneath him. Josh stood slowly. He turned away from the grisly scene and shut his eyes. He had to think.

"Josh," Shannon whispered. "What can we do?"

He opened his eyes and saw her staring up at him. "Can you find the place where we told Dad we'd meet him?" he asked.

She nodded. "I think so."

"Follow our tracks. Look for the tall spruce. He should be waiting there. Tell him to bring the machine, and the sled, to the top of the ravine. Only not too close. We don't want to draw her out again."

"What about Nathan?"

"I'm going to try to bring him around the bend, where the bear can't see us. Get the bleeding stopped."

"But what if—what if she comes after you, too?"

Josh glanced back at the den. "That's a chance I'll have to take. Can't just watch him lie there and bleed to death. I'll go slow and hope she's busy nursing those cubs."

She shook her head. "I don't like it. It's too dangerous."

"Shannon, please. I need your help. And every minute counts. It's a long way to the clinic."

She hesitated, then turned and began to pick her way back along their tracks. He followed her with his eyes until she disappeared beyond the trees. He could only hope she paid attention and recognized the meeting spot.

Josh looked back at his brother's crumpled body. Crimson patches spread in the snow beneath him. Josh breathed deep. He took a step into the snow. The wind-blown surface crunched before his boot sank into the muffling powder below. He glanced toward the den but saw no movement. He stepped again, this time easing his boot through the surface, so it made only a faint scraping sound as it plunged into the snow.

Josh looked around the bend and fixed his eyes on his brother. The den, dark and menacing, loomed beyond. He took first one concentrated step and then another until he had rounded the bend and was in open view of the bear, should she emerge again.

Even in the cold, Josh felt a trickle of sweat run down the side of his neck. One step at a time, he told himself. He tried to forget the terrible animal that could strike at any moment and forced himself to concentrate on his brother. He willed himself closer. One step, and then another. His heart pounded louder with each one.

When at last he reached Nathan, Josh knelt beside him in the snow. His brother's eyes were closed, his face frozen in pain.

Josh felt the panic rise in his throat. He pulled off his glove and stretched his trembling hand toward his brother's cheek. It was still warm. He put a finger under his nose and felt the warmth of his shallow breath.

With one eye on the den, Josh looked over Nathan's mangled arms and shoulder. He needed first to slow the bleeding. Josh threw off his parka and removed his flannel shirt. As he wrapped the flannel tightly around the torn shoulder and down the arm, his brother's eyelids flickered.

"Lie still," Josh whispered. "Got to get you out of here."

Josh pulled his long john top over his head. He barely felt the cold air hit his chest. He wrapped the cotton top swiftly, binding the gaping flesh of the other arm. Blood already saturated the flannel of the first dressing.

He reached for his parka, and at the same instant he heard a rustle that drew his eyes in terror to the den. But it was only a gust of wind sweeping through the birch branches high overhead.

Nathan lay with eyes now open. Josh could clearly see the pain they held. He knelt at his brother's side.

"Nathan, I've got to try to drag you around the

bend." Josh swallowed hard. It was a huge risk. If the bear had broken bones in Nathan's neck or back, he might never walk again. Josh looked back at the dark opening of the den. The danger of waiting here was even greater.

His brother winced in pain as Josh gently lifted his arms to his chest, crossing them at the wrists. Josh stepped out of one of his boots and pulled off a sock, using it to bind Nathan's wrists together. Then he tucked his bare foot back into the boot.

Nathan's face looked nearly as pale as the snow in which he lay. Josh leaned over him and whispered. "I'm going to grab on to your legs. I'll keep an eye on your face. You let me know if it hurts too bad."

His brother nodded weakly and shut his eyes. Josh lifted Nathan's boots and grasped his ankles. He tugged, walking backward, one slow step at a time. Nathan's parka glided almost silently across the snow.

Josh looked from his brother's face to the open den as he took step after cautious step backward. Nathan's mouth was contorted with pain, but his lips were pressed firmly together. The den gaped dark and silent.

One step, and then another. At last he reached the bend, stepping out and around it. Then he knelt at Nathan's side. Breathing hard, he pulled off his glove and touched his brother's face. Nathan's eyes fluttered open.

"Thanks." His mouth formed the word without voice. Then his eyes closed.

Josh sat back in the snow, listening for the dreaded sound of the bear emerging once more—or for the welcome sound of a snow machine racing toward the ravine. But he heard only the cry of a raven in the distance and the labored sound of his own breathing.

A shiver ran through his body as the damp inside of his parka pressed against his bare chest. There was nothing to do now but wait—wait and hope that Shannon had made it back to the tall spruce and to his father.

15

$\mathcal{F}$INALLY, he heard the machine. It drew closer and closer to the ravine, coming to a stop just above where Josh waited beside his brother.

His father scrambled down the embankment. "My God!" he exclaimed when he saw Nathan, his arms and shoulder wrapped in Josh's blood-soaked shirts.

"I think we can carry him up to the machine. I dragged him around that bend, away from the den. It didn't seem to hurt him too much."

"Got to try," his father said. Worry shone in his eyes. "Looks like he's lost a lot of blood."

Josh nodded. He lifted Nathan at the feet while his father took the shoulders. "It's going to be all right, Nate," he heard his father say. "We're going to get you out of here."

They stumbled up the bank to the machine and sled at the top. In the sled were two sleeping bags.

"Shannon's idea," his father explained as he unrolled and unzipped the bags.

Josh had to give her credit for clear thinking. His own thoughts were starting to blur. He helped his father hoist Nathan into the sled and zip one bag around his shivering form. They laid the other bag on top and tucked it around him.

His father drove fast. Josh stared straight ahead, picking out landmarks that seemed too far apart. Only once did he turn and look at Nathan. Tucked under the bags, he looked small and helpless. The grayish tint of his skin made Josh catch his breath and turn away.

Frank, Pete, and Shannon burst from their cabin door before the machine even pulled to a stop. Frank's truck was parked beside theirs, and both vehicles were running. Shannon and her dad helped Josh and his father lift Nathan, sleeping bags and all, into the front seat of their pickup while Pete looked on, wide-eyed.

"Have you loosened his clothing?" Shannon asked. The frightened look had left her eyes, and her tone was matter-of-fact.

Josh shook his head.

"We need to." Already she was unzipping the bag and reaching to unlace his boots.

She looked over the wrappings Josh had used to bind Nathan's arms and shoulder. "Those look good. Just a little fresh blood, from when we lifted him. Best to leave them, I think."

Where had she learned all of this? Maybe in school. There were no first-aid lessons in Josh's correspondence materials.

Josh climbed in the passenger side of the truck, cradling his brother's head in his lap. His father got behind the wheel, and Shannon brought a pillow from their truck to prop Nathan's feet.

"We'll follow right behind," Frank yelled as they pulled away.

His father drove fast, pushing the old truck harder than Josh would have thought possible. Josh stared at the road that would take them to Wasilla. Only hours before, he had anticipated a joyous journey down this road, toward a new life. Now the journey was filled with fear and apprehension, and the life in question was his brother's.

Every few miles, Josh touched Nathan's face. His gray skin felt cool and clammy, and his breathing was rapid and shallow. Nathan's eyes remained closed. The memory of the look those eyes had held just before the bear moved in, the look of shock, of betrayal even, hung in Josh's mind.

A wave of relief came over Josh when at last they squealed around a corner and into the parking lot of the Wasilla Clinic. The emergency team whisked Nathan into a room in the back, and his father followed. Josh sank into a chair in the waiting room and hung his head in his hands.

He felt the weight of a thin arm on his shoulder, drawing him close. A fresh, soap-clean smell.

Shannon said nothing. She just sat, her arm on his shoulder.

Josh remembered her earlier words, reassuring him about Nathan. "He's fine." But then she'd spoken only of his shelter from the cold. That was before all of this bloodshed.

He looked up at the sound of the waiting-room door. Frank came in, with Pete holding on to one hand.

"Any news?" Frank asked.

Josh shook his head. "Not yet. They've got him back there. Dad's with him."

Pete was strangely silent. He took a step toward Josh, but Frank stopped him, directing him toward a chair. Frank whispered something in his ear, and Pete picked up a kid's magazine from the end table.

Josh sat forward, his elbows on his knees. "I just don't get it," he said in a low voice.

"What?" Shannon asked.

"How Nathan was there, all of a sudden, with that bear."

"I think—I think maybe he crawled out of her den." She dropped her arm from his shoulder.

"Out of her den?" Anger rose in his voice. Hanging around a bear den was suicidal. "What was he thinking?"

"He seemed like he felt a sort of, well, kinship with that bear. Almost a mystical thing. When he found that empty den, he said he felt like he belonged there."

A memory came to Josh—the look of rage in Nathan's eyes, back in October, when he realized the bear had been mortally wounded. "My brother," he had said accusingly. He'd meant the bear.

"He told you all of this?" Josh asked.

She nodded. "I followed his tracks and found him in the empty den. We talked. First just about Thoreau and stuff. Then he got going on the bears. He said he thought I'd understand."

Josh imagined the two of them, huddled in the darkness of the abandoned den. He flexed his hands, then clenched them into fists. "Did you? Did you understand?"

Shannon studied him a moment. "Sort of. I understood him wanting to be close to nature. Even feeling that close to an animal. And the empty den was a warm, safe place. I think he was trying to get in touch with a part of himself there."

Slowly, Josh released his tense grip. "But why move from there into a den with a hibernating bear?"

She shook her head. "He showed me the fresh den last time I talked to him. It was like this treasure he had uncovered. But I had no idea he'd try to get inside. Maybe it was like the ultimate test. Or maybe he just got cold."

Josh looked Shannon in the eye. "You could have said something about a bear before we went near that second den."

She looked away. "I know," she said softly. "I realize that now. But when Nathan talked about the bears, he made them sound so—so honorable. And when he'd shown me the den before, the bear was out cold, hibernating."

"But Nathan knows plenty about bears." Josh felt the irritation rise in his voice. "Surely he knows they can wake from hibernation, even in the dead of winter. Surely he knows the risk of getting anywhere near a sow nursing newborn cubs."

"I'm not sure any kind of risk would stop your brother," Shannon said quietly.

Josh stood abruptly. He took a few steps to the tiny window of the waiting area and stood, staring out into the winter gray. If only he hadn't yelled his brother's name. Deep down, he knew that the bear most likely hadn't wakened by accident. His voice, or his brother moving in response to it, would have startled her. And once she sensed the potential danger to her cubs . . . it was a wonder she hadn't torn Nathan to pieces.

Josh's father came through the swinging door of the emergency area. Frank looked up from his magazine. "How is he?"

"They've stabilized him," Josh's father replied. "For the transport to Anchorage, by ambulance." His voice was low, unsteady.

Stabilized. It didn't mean much. Josh got up and stood beside his father. "Let's go, then," he said quietly.

In the truck, Josh's father stared grimly ahead, watching the traffic. Cars filled the lanes around them. The ambulance, lights flashing, had passed them miles back, and they could no longer hear the fading siren.

It was strange, Josh thought aimlessly. Nathan hated technology, but now his life depended on the speeding ambulance and the high-tech hospital. Nathan, who wanted above all to prove himself, to be in control, had been rendered helpless in a matter of minutes.

Josh looked at his father, whose face was set as if in stone. Driving to Wasilla, he'd asked Josh the basics of the attack, and he'd listened without response. Did he understand the horror Josh had felt? The fear at trying to bring Nathan to safety with the bear close at hand? Did he appreciate what Josh had done, or did he blame him as Josh was beginning to blame himself? The questions swirled in Josh's mind.

They stopped at Mountain View Drive, the first light on the edge of Anchorage. Josh watched the cars move through the intersection. Each driver looked intent on a destination. When they'd lived in Anchorage, he used to study the drivers, trying to imagine where each one might be going. If someone tried to guess where he and his father were going now, Josh knew they'd miss the mark. He could scarcely believe it himself.

"Did they say what they'd do when they got him to the hospital?" Josh asked.

"A complete evaluation," his father replied. "Probably surgery."

Josh tried to think of some comforting words he could say to his father. Nathan would be fine. No, they didn't know that. The doctors would take good care of him. But what did Josh know about the doctors at Providence Hospital?

They pulled away from the light with no comforting words from Josh. It was as if the burden of standing between his father and Nathan had suddenly grown far too heavy to carry any longer. Josh felt the weight of the emotions from the last few hours press upon him—disappointment, horror, anger, uncertainty.

A school bus pulled to a stop in front of them, its red lights flashing. Josh's father tapped his fingers impatiently on the dash while they waited for the bus to unload.

High school students, getting off at their stop after a day at school, spilled out of the bus's double doors, laughing and talking, swinging their book bags. Soon they'd be home, opening the refrigerator door for a snack, turning on the TV, calling friends on the phone to talk over the day. Living normal lives.

A normal life. Through the confusion of the moment, the uncertainty about Nathan, Josh felt his resolution grow strong. No matter how all of this turned out, he had to get back to a normal life, a life in town, where he'd go to school and have friends and maybe play hockey again. Once they got through this crisis, he had to insist. His father could let Nathan run his life, but Josh had to start running his own.

The bus closed its doors. As soon as its red lights went off, Josh's father hit the gas and pulled around it. The gray façade of Providence Hospital loomed in the distance.

Josh looked once more at his father's anxious face, caught up in worry over his older son. Josh looked away. Now more than ever, Nathan controlled their lives.

16

$\mathcal{T}$HE HOSPITAL'S EMERGENCY WAITING ROOM was much like the clinic's, only bigger. Fluorescent lights flickered overhead, and low music filtered from unseen speakers. His father joined the surgeon in the pre-op room for a brief consultation.

Josh picked up a magazine and flipped through it aimlessly. Schoolgirls modeling bright spring shades of makeup smiled at him from the pages. He closed the magazine and looked up.

Shannon stood at his side. She shrugged off her jacket and sat beside him. "Dad took Pete home. He felt like this was too much for him."

Josh nodded.

"But he said I could stay. I hope you don't mind."

"Suit yourself," Josh said. "I guess you're worried about Nathan."

"And you. That was a horrible experience."

Josh said nothing. The buzzing of the lights seemed to grow louder.

"Pulling him away from the den," she went on. "You must have been terrified."

Josh shrugged. "I guess."

Shannon got up and walked to the window. She stood, staring out over the city. Josh looked in her direction, but he stayed in his seat.

Finally she turned and walked briskly toward where he sat, until she stood looking down at him. "Look, Josh," she said. "I know you want to move back to town. If you're going to live around people, you can't just shut them out whenever you please."

Josh stood and walked to a rack of magazines. An urgent voice came over the intercom. "Dr. Henley to emergency, please. Dr. Henley to emergency."

He put a hand out and leaned his weight against the wall. The sounds and the bright lights seemed overwhelming.

Shannon came to his side. "Talk to me," she persisted.

Josh rubbed his forehead. The quiet of the cabin, tucked away in miles of undisturbed snow, welcomed him in his mind, and for a moment he couldn't think of why he had wanted so desperately to leave.

He felt Shannon set her hand on his shoulder. "I'm here for you," she said quietly. "Talk to me."

Josh turned and looked at her. "About what?" he conceded.

"Anything. You. Your father. Your half brother. How you got here. Where you're going."

"OK, that's enough," he interrupted. A slight smile formed on his lips.

They sat. At first the words flowed slowly. She asked about his childhood, and he told her about Chicago, about the apartment and their neighbors, about his mother's growing restlessness. Then before he knew it, he'd told her about how his mother left and how his father had sunk into a deep depression.

"It was like my dad needed me, even though I was only eight," Josh said.

"You must have missed your mother," Shannon said.

"I did, a lot. At first she'd call, and she'd get me on weekends. But Dad told me she wanted her freedom, and I guess she did, because once she started dating this guy from out of town, it was like she never looked back." Josh paused. Even though it had been so long ago, it still hurt to talk about it.

Just then his father emerged from his talk with the surgeon.

"They're cleaning him up for surgery right now," he explained. "They've got an artery to repair and some skin to transplant. But his vital signs are improving. The doctor says his chances are good."

He paused and put a hand on Josh's shoulder. "And the doctor said your bandaging probably saved his life."

"That's good, Dad," Josh said. But at that moment, his father's hand on his shoulder felt especially heavy.

"I should call my father," Shannon said. "Just to let him know."

She went off to the pay phone, and Josh was alone with his dad.

"So they're sure he'll be all right?" Josh asked.

"Pretty sure. Of course, there's always a risk with surgery. And they don't know till they get in there how much damage there has been to the arm and shoulder muscles. He may not regain full use of them."

"That would be hard for Nathan, not to be able to do everything for himself," Josh said.

"It would," his father agreed.

Josh took a deep breath. "But then again, doing everything for himself got Nathan into this mess. Got all of us into this mess."

His father sat. He stroked at his beard, as he did whenever he was thinking. Finally he spoke. "I guess you're right," he said softly.

Shannon came back from the phone. "Dad said to tell you he's glad for the good news so far. He said to call when Nathan gets out of surgery. He'll come pick me up then, with my mom and Pete. Oh, and Mom said you two are welcome to stay with us while Nathan's in the hospital."

Josh's father smiled. "Much obliged. We'll be needing a place to stay for a while, till we can figure out where to go from here."

Josh knew where he was going, and it wasn't far. He'd stay in town and try to get on with his life. Whether his father went along or not didn't matter anymore. He'd figure out a way. He could get in touch with old friends, guys from his team. Someone's family would help him out.

"Did they say how long he'd be in surgery?" Shannon asked.

"Two or three hours," Josh's father replied.

"In that case, maybe we should go down to the cafeteria or something," she suggested. "For a change of scene."

Josh half smiled. She had a bit of the same restless spirit that drove Nathan, always looking for a change. "Sounds good to me," he said.

Josh's father shook his head. "You two go on. I think I'll wait here a while. Maybe go downstairs to the chapel."

Josh hesitated. Perhaps his father needed him just now, especially if he was thinking about the chapel. His father hadn't set foot in a church since they'd left Chicago.

He thought back over his earlier words with Shannon. His father had needed him back when he was eight and they had only each other. But now he had Nathan, and Josh had his own plans. His father would have to sort things out for himself.

"It's a strange thing," Josh said. He sat across from Shannon in the hospital cafeteria, sipping at a cup of bitter coffee. "I couldn't wait to get to town. Now this. I guess I'll be in town all right, but it won't be like I was expecting."

Shannon stirred her hot chocolate. "Nothing ever turns out like we expect, does it?"

Josh turned the heavy cup in his hands. "I guess not. I just thought things would be more normal if Dad and I got out of Willow Creek."

Shannon caught his eye, and for a moment it seemed as if she was looking into his innermost self. Josh felt hot in his parka, but he couldn't remove it, not without a shirt or even long johns underneath. Instead, he reached to unzip the coat a bit, breaking Shannon's gaze.

"Willow Creek's a special place," Shannon said softly.

Josh shifted in the hard plastic chair and looked back at her. "I know. It hasn't been all horrible. But it's lonely."

"Lonely isn't necessarily bad."

"It is when it's forced on you, when you have no alternative. After a while, you start to wonder if you'd still know how to have friends, if you'd fit in some-where else."

"But you have your dad and Nathan."

Josh drew in a deep breath. "Don't get me wrong—I love my dad. For a long time we had only each other. Then he found Nathan, and everything changed."

"But for the better, right? You'd been looking all those years, and then you found him."

"Dad was looking. When he found him, Nathan seemed like just another guy to me. Not like a brother. Not like Pete is a brother to you. I mean, I didn't grow up with him. We didn't have much in common. But Dad was so drawn to him. Nathan would get to talking about something, and Dad would get all worked up about it, too."

Shannon nodded. "I can see that. Nathan has a way about him. You know that he thinks for himself and lives what he believes."

Josh pushed the coffee cup aside. "Without regard for anyone else."

"But Nathan has a deep regard for nature and her creatures."

"A deep regard for nature, maybe, but not much for common sense. Look where that's gotten him. That's one reason why Dad couldn't let go of Nathan after he found him, why we had to follow him into the wilderness. He worried about him."

Josh took a deep breath. "Not me, though. I was willing to let Nathan seal his fate with his crazy ideas."

"Still, today, when he was in danger, you saved his life."

Josh let her words sink in. "I did what anyone would have done. And maybe I did feel something for Nathan today that I've never felt before, something like a brother should feel. But still, it's not my place to keep saving Nathan from himself. Dad can do that. Not me."

"No matter what happens with you and your dad and Nathan, you'll always have Willow Creek," Shannon said.

Willow Creek. It wasn't exactly a source of comfort, after all he'd been through.

"Like I said, from the first time we visited Willow Creek, I knew it was a special place," she continued. "I loved the wildness of it all."

Josh let his mind go back to the cabin they'd built from logs they'd cut and peeled themselves, to the cellar with meat they'd put up for the winter. And beyond the cabin, the stands of scraggly spruce and willow, the spreading sky, the mountains rising up in the distance. There was an undeniable beauty mixed with the harsh reality.

"It was hard to leave, even knowing I'd be back," Shannon continued. "But I had this thought, this thought that once you've been in the wilderness, a part of it will always be with you."

Josh looked away from Shannon, toward the cafeteria window. Above the lights that twinkled in the growing dusk, the snow-streaked Chugach Mountains loomed. Beyond, miles of empty wilderness stretched in all directions. And somewhere in that vast expanse, nestled at the foot of the Alaska Range, was their tiny cabin at Willow Creek, where he'd spent the two hardest years of his life. And he knew she was right. No matter where he went, no matter what he did, a part of the wilderness would be with him always.